The White Twilight

Books by Madeleine Polland

BY MADELEINE POLLAND

The White Twilight

ILLUSTRATED BY ALAN COBER

HOLT, RINEHART AND WINSTON

NEW YORK / CHICAGO / SAN FRANCISCO

The White Twilight

There was ice between the cobbles in the streets of Antwerp, glittering hard and brilliant in the dark stones, though it was only mid-October. The high round gables of the rich houses were black against a pale clear frosty sky and from their vast unshuttered windows the light fell warm as amber into the icy dusk. Below their high walls, wooden pattens clacked sharply along the street and two young girls came walking home from school. Their colored mantles glowed in the frosty shadows, and behind them the round face of their serving woman was scarlet with the cold.

"Hanne, I am truly sorry that you have to go away."

It was the smaller one who spoke, looking up affectionately at her friend; but Hanne did not look back at her. She kept her heavy-lidded eyes on the slippery cobbles and her wide mouth curved in a small satisfied smile. She was tall and very thin, in spite of the bulk of her heavy mantle, and her fair hair was banded smooth and neat along the edge of her cap below the warm furred hood.

"I am twelve now," she said calmly, "and my father says he needs me. I am to be his companion and care for him. I am quite old enough, and my Aunt Elena has taught me all I need to know of being a good housekeeper." Her light voice was prim and certain, and Margrit glanced at her again. Nothing ever seemed to excite Hanne. She was so *quiet!* Perhaps she had lived too long alone with her Aunt Elena, who—as everybody knew—was the most house-proud woman in all Antwerp; polishing her great dark shining house from dawn to sunset and stopping only for her prayers! Cheerfully Margrit pushed a straggle of hair back under her half-tied hood and, where a button had fallen off the front, held her crimson cloak together against the wind. Her small round face grew bright with pleasure as she thought again of where her friend was going.

"To a castle," she breathed for the thousandth time. "To live in a real king's castle, and while the King is living there himself. You are fortunate, Hanne."

"Yes." Even Hanne's cool empty voice warmed a little at the thought. "I am to have rooms with my father. The King, he says, is very kind, and the Queen is beautiful and charming. They have three children."

"How long has your father been in Kron—Kron?" Margrit never tired of going over it all.

"Kronborg," Hanne said carefully. "It is outside a little town called Elsinore, on the east coast of the eastern island of Denmark, called Zeeland. I asked our tutor to show it to me on the globe."

Margrit's cheerful mouth pulled itself into a square. Hanne could make even an adventure like this into a school lesson. How she wished it were she, going off across the frosty land to the strange northern seas of Denmark. She would ask no tutor! She would come back and tell him all about it!

"My father has been gone four years," Hanne went on, and it was impossible to tell if she were sad. "King Frederick of Denmark appointed him his architect in 1577. He came back just for a time, to engage all his craftsmen."

Margrit sniffed in the cold air and rubbed a mittened hand

§11

on her frozen nose. Her skin felt raw under the rasp of the icy wool. Hanne's mind was full of household lists and the care of the few chambers that would be her father's home. Her small friend sighed and thought of the wonder and excitement of the great castle rising under the skill of Master van Maebergen beside the cold distant Danish sea. Would Hanne ever see it, or would she be thinking all the time about the cost of cheese? She laughed at herself and then turned to kiss Hanne good-bye outside the tall oak gates of her aunt's house.

"God be with you, Hanne," she said. "I shall be waiting for you to tell me all about it when you come back from your adventure. Give my duty to your Aunt Elena and my wishes for a safe journey."

"My adventure?" Hanne picked out the word, and her fair eyebrows lifted. Under the great iron lantern which hung above the gate, her hair shone smooth and bright under her hood, and her long serious face seemed untouched by the cold that nipped Margrit's round cheeks to scarlet and brought tears to the eyes of the waiting servant. Pale and cool, she bent and kissed her untidy little friend.

"Good-bye, Margrit. And what adventure can I have? There will be no adventure in being a good and suitable companion to my father."

Margrit shook her head at her and then gathered up her gown and scampered off along the shadow of the wall toward her own home. Hanne tidied her disturbed hood and waited patiently for the serving woman to open the big double gate.

Dawn was gray and bitter across the sleeping city as she

came into the courtyard the next morning for the start of their long journey. The icy air was white with the blown breath of the horses and the frost crisp under their restless hooves. She was still calm and quiet, listening without answer to the fret and bustle of her elderly aunt, who pattered here and there among the train of servants in the torchlight, her huge cloak billowing like a sail; checking this and altering that and pausing every now and then to look in fresh anxiety at the icy sky where the stars paled above the gables.

At last she stopped beside her niece and shook her head.

"Hanne, my child, I am afraid. Never in my life have I seen it so cold so early. We have weeks of traveling before us. What if winter should catch us still on the road? I wonder if we shouldn't wait until the spring. It is not too late to change our minds." She looked helplessly at the crowded courtyard as if she did not really believe this last. Her usually severe and certain face was crumpled with anxiety, and the crimped linen creaked about her long neck as she turned her face upward and looked this way and that, as though she might get an answer from the cold lightening sky. But it was Hanne who answered her, no longer calm and quiet; long heavy eyes wide open in fright and dismay. The icy air caught her throat and she coughed and spluttered at her aunt.

"No! No, Aunt Elena, no. We promised to be with my father for the Christmas Feast! We must go now. We are all ready!" She flapped a frantic hand at the laden horses. "We can't undo all this."

Yesterday she had bidden all her friends good-bye, calmly superior because she was traveling all the long strange way

to Denmark to live with her father in the castle of a king while they would come back the same as every other day, to their childish desks. They had gathered round her, wide-eyed and respectful, and Hanne had felt important and secure. She was going to her father. How could she go back now like all the rest of them and take her place below the tutor's chair, and have to tell them that she was not going? They would laugh at her, and that she couldn't bear. They laughed enough already because they said she was a prig.

"No, no, Aunt Elena, we must go as we have planned."

Her hands were clenched tight inside her big furred sleeves.

In the flickering torchlight that slowly lost its scarlet to the brightening day, Aunt Elena looked in astonishment at the tense young face.

"Your affection for your father does you credit. I am surprised you remember him so well."

Hanne blinked. She looked almost bewildered. Remember him well?

"Very well, child." Aunt Elena patted her on the shoulder and then lifted a hand to the watching servants. Once more the bustle rose among the laden horses. "Piet the gardener tells me I need not be afraid," she went on. "We will believe him. He says it will soon be mild enough again to get us safe to Kronborg, and he is always right about the weather. No, no, Jan, that does not go there!" She was off again among the pack train, waving urgent hands towards a servant, and Hanne stood quite still. The frosty sun had risen now and the sky glowed above the red brick gables. In front of her, the courtyard was bright with sudden color, warming cold faces into life, and the smoke of the quenched torches crept up black and straight into the still air. She was thinking of her father.

That Aunt Elena could think she might forget him! It was for him that she must always be perfect; always the best; always do what was right. Then she might grow good and clever enough for this brilliant, famous father to take notice of her. She sighed. He was kind and easy with her, and liked to have her near him. Had he not sent for her to join him in Kronborg? But he never saw her. He looked straight through her with busy kindness, and out of the other side of her to the gable of some castle or the spire of some church that filled his mind. That was why she wanted to be his house-keeper. It was not enough to be his daughter. She must struggle to be useful and grown-up and always good, and then he might really see her. He never saw a child. She sighed again and jumped as her aunt's sharp voice reached her across the court. The trampled frost was dark and wet now on the red tiles, and the long train of horses stood ready to move off.

"Do we all stand waiting for your dreaming? Come, child, we are ready to go."

A servant helped Hanne mount her horse, and the old woman who had nursed her from a baby came over to wrap a fur-lined cloak about her legs, close against the bitter wind that whistled through the gateway opened to the street. Hanne kissed the cold withered cheek as she bade her nurse good-bye, and for a moment her calm face crumpled and tears welled hot and unhappy behind her eyes. Then she straightened firmly in her saddle; past childhood, past tears.

§16

At the head of the long train of baggage horses, guards, and servants, she clattered behind her aunt through the great archway and out into the still quiet morning city. The cobbles were white in the untrodden street and the horses slipped and clacked and struggled for a grip as they turned and headed out towards the northwest and the great half-built castle of Kronborg.

CHAPTER TWO

Piet the gardener was right. For the most of the long weeks of
their journey the skies were mild and wide and the weather
soft. Across the flat unending plains of Holland and over the
wide blue Rhine at Arnhem; through the thick darkness of
the German forests and on over the ghostly wastes of Lune-
burg, where the menservants rode with pistols cocked for
highwaymen and the wind moaned like a phantom in the
trees. They stayed a while to rest at Hamburg, lodging in
warm comfort with relatives of Aunt Elena, and at Kiel,
Master van Maebergen had arranged for them to take ship
for Copenhagen. But before they reached there, the mild
weather changed; the skies grew hard and dark and the bitter
cold once more wrapped all the north of Europe.

The voyage from Kiel was a lurching nightmare of cold and
wind and creaking timbers and the sour smell of fear and
sickness. In the bright icy morning at the end of it, Hanne
crept from the cabin full of moaning women and struggled to
the deck to look for Copenhagen. They were already inside
the long narrow harbor, but even here the sea was flayed by a
bitter wind and ice hung in fingers from the shrouds. The air
she gulped so gladly was cold as pain in her throat, but she
forgot the cold in her pleasure in the city that waited for her
at the harbor end. She thought of all the old tales she had
been told when she was small, when she would sit before
the parlor fire with her nurse and listen in the dusk to tales
of ancient fairy cities and imprisoned princesses and fair
knights and wicked dragons. She did not know why Copen-

hagen made her think of this. It looked as if it might vanish
if she looked away, lying there so lightly at the end of its
long water, icy blue in the winter sun.

She smiled and she did look away and Copenhagen did
not vanish. It came slowly closer, until at last the ship drew
in below the quay, and above her she could see her father's
servants waiting, old friends from the days beside the parlor
fire. As soon as the plank was down, she forgot poor Aunt
Elena and struggled ashore, gathering up her skirts to climb
the sea-wet icy steps where the ship had berthed.

"Hans!" she cried. "Georg!" Her tired sedate face was
suddenly a child's again as she took the hands of the elderly
man who had been the family steward since her father's
boyhood and smiled at his son, who had care of all Master
van Maebergen's horses.

"Mistress Hanne! You are so grown!" The old man's face
was alight with pleasure. "Kronborg will be home to Master
Julius when he has his child again."

Hanne's pleased face dimmed and took on its closed look.
Hans let go her fingers and eased himself down the icy steps.
"First now we must care for your aunt. I doubt she has
enjoyed her voyage."

The girl turned back to the old lady, who struggled onto
the deck of the ship between the arms of her serving women,
her thin face still green with the agonies of her journey.
Hanne's conscience touched her. She wanted nothing but to
leave her aunt and get on to Kronborg. How could she be so
unkind to Aunt Elena, who in her strict way had always been
so kind to her! But Hanne wanted to rush on to the new
world of being grown-up, where she might impress her father,

and Aunt Elena belonged to the world of childhood; of being told what to do. Hanne grudged the few weeks they were to spend in Copenhagen, visiting with yet another of her father's sisters.

"Mistress Hanne! Do you listen?"

She turned her abstracted eyes to Hans, who spoke to her for the second time.

"Mistress Hanne, I am trying to tell you we have changed our plans. Your father is anxious about the weather. We are to take you on to Kronborg at once, when we have lodged Mistress van Maebergen with her sister here. Your father will bring you to visit them in the spring, but feels it better that you travel on to Kronborg immediately, lest you are snowbound here in Copenhagen. You understand?"

He thought the child looked vague and confused. Tired no doubt. She looked too old, somehow. No life for a child, all these years alone with that old woman. Ah well, not his business. He scratched under the edge of his cap, where sparse gray hair protruded, and looked at the sky above the harbor. It had lost its brightness now and hung like lead above the crowded ships and the city spires, stilling the color of the cold sea and loosing an occasional large flake of snow to drift down and lie unmelted on their clothes.

"I will explain to your aunt," he said, "and we will ride at once for Elsinore. We have no time to lose, if we are to be there before the snow."

Hanne was bewildered by the sudden speed of their journey, and saw in the strange lovely city only a confusion of streets and waterways and tall houses with strange steep sloping roofs.

"They get much snow here," Hans explained, "and the steep roofs help it to slide off."

Hanne stared. "Will my father build the castle with steep roofs such as these?"

"But of course."

Hanne stored the fact away. Something she could say one day to her father; something she would know that he had not told her.

By noon they were well to the north of the city, deep in the forest where the huge spreading beeches mixed with the tall firs to close the sky above their heads, and all the green twilight of the day was filled with silence and the threat of the oncoming snow. Hanne peered now and then through the tall crowding trunks of the trees.

"Hans. We are following the sea."

"Yes, Mistress Hanne. Kronborg stands on the sea."

"I know. Why then did we not go all the way by ship?"

"The narrow seas up here can be most dangerous in winter. Your father felt you both would have had enough sea voyaging by now, and he thought your aunt would be more comfortable in the city for a time."

In a clearing of the forest he lifted his thoughtful face to the sky, and the girl followed his eyes. There was no snow yet, but the sky was dark and solid, resting like a threat above the stripped trees. By the time the early dusk was thickening over the glimpses of the sea, the snow had come. They had left the thickest part of the forest, and open wooded country stretched away on either side of their road, but soon it was lost in the white whirling confusion that came at first stealthily in deadly quiet, creeping down a few flakes at a time to melt on the warm coats of the horses. Then it fell faster, and across the flat country the wind rose and took it in clouds, swirling snow in frenzied flurries from all sides of them until it seemed to come up from the very ground itself. Hans and Georg closed in on both sides of Hanne and each took one of her reins with his own.

"Hold to your bridle, little Mistress!" yelled Hans above the keening wind, and she eased her fast-freezing fingers from the reins and bent above her horse's head.

The strange eerie dusk passed quickly, and then there was nothing but thick snow-filled darkness; nothing at all except the fast-vanishing feeling of the bridle between her numb fingers, and the rub of Georg's leg against her own; only the cold confusing wetness plastering her face and running in bitter icy trickles down the inside of her mantle. And through all the wild white darkness, the unlikely warmth and the safe familiar smell of the horses that she could not even see. Deep in her stomach grew a cold patch of creeping fear as remorseless as the snow itself, but she refused to show it, biting her lips and blinking fiercely so that she might stare blindly into the whirling cloud as if she could see.

Finally they stopped, and Hanne pulled frantically on her bridle to keep herself from falling forward as her exhausted horse dropped his head before the biting wind. Hans and Georg could not even see her.

"Father!" yelled Georg across her in the darkness. "Where are we?"

"I don't know, Georg. I don't know. I feel branches on my face at times, but if we were on the right road, we should not now be in the forest!"

Their voices were thin and helpless in the wind.

Hanne raised her head and peered through the snow that froze to her lashes. Through the gusts that tore apart the snow, she could just make out the close shadow of trees, so black and dense they must be pines, weighted already with their burden of white. She shook her head, fighting her longing for sleep; longing to let go the icy bridle and slide off the horse; to let her heavy eyes close, and stay closed.

"Get on!" yelled Hans again. "We *must* keep moving! Come, little Mistress. You will be safe with Hans. Come with Hans."

She could barely see the glimmer of his snow-crusted face, but there was safety and comfort in the old familiar voice, speaking as he had spoken when she was small; as though they were safe in the bright warm rooms of her father's house and he was coaxing her to some childish duty. Tears threatened for a moment, hot and strange on her lashes, and then she forced them back and crouched again over her horses's head, feeling the warm rise of his breath on her face in the darkness.

They had long lost count of the hours and the wind had risen to a gale as they plodded on, guiding themselves by the thick trees which kept them to some track. Fierce gusts tore the snow apart into moments of clear darkness and in one of these Hans shouted suddenly, his man's voice thin like a child's.

"Georg! I saw a light!"

"I, too," Hanne tried to say, but no voice would come.

Then Georg shouted, and for a moment the light was clear, showing bright and certain in the white whirling turmoil. Then it was lost again as the wind drove back the snow. But at last it was a window. Snow drifted round its edges, and the dark bulk of a house loomed suddenly above them. Then Hanne cried and could not stop, and remembered very little more but her own hot tears on her face, and fingers pulling her frozen hands from her bridle, and strong arms that seemed to carry her up steps.

Long after, she sat alone in a vast cushioned chair before a stove, waking gradually to the strange warm comfortable room and the terrifying memory of the snow. She did not know where she was, and she was still too weary to care. The blue and white flowers on the tiles of the glowing stove seemed to weave and dance before her drowsy eyes, and the candles blurred and swelled in the candlesticks on the polished table. She slipped into her cushions and slept again.

When next she woke she was startled to see a man standing by her chair. She had not heard him come. There was no door to the room, only an arch, opening to the next one, and he had come in silence. Hans and Georg would not have left her if there was anything to fear; and this man did not look evil. There was even something in his dress and bearing that made her want to struggle to her feet to show him her manners, and make him a formal curtsy. As she groped with the folds of the long fur robe that wrapped her, the man smiled and laid a hand on her shoulder, easing her back.

"Tomorrow will do for manners, Mistress van Maebergen. You have had a bad frightening journey. Rest now and be warm."

His voice was slow and lazy and she could easily understand him. She had been learning Danish for two years, to prepare for the time that she would join her father. The man drew up a round three-legged stool, and sat down companionably beside her.

"Your men tell me you are the child of Julius van Maebergen, who works on Kronborg."

"Yes, sir." She felt sure that she should call him "sir," even though she could only half see him in the soft rosy light; only the turn of his square chin and the sheen of the dark hair that fell to his ruff. Pride rose in her again and the fierce longing to be worthy of her famous father.

"I go to Kronborg to be his housekeeper."

The man held out his hands to the stove, and turned at the tired prim voice. As he looked at the thin child in the great carved chair, she caught the gleam of his eyes and the smile that touched his mouth.

"So?" he said, and she could not think why he should be amused.

She was remembering her manners now, and all the careful training of Aunt Elena. "I have to thank you, sir," she said in her careful Danish, "for the way you have helped me and my father's men. We are most grateful. I thank you, sir—Mynheer——?"

"Count," he said. "Count," Again the amusement touched his face. "Count Andreas af Rosenborg. At your service, Mistress——?"

Hanne looked at him, sharp and suspicious and on her dignity. She thought he was laughing at her and she didn't like it. She hated to be laughed at. Her long Flemish face was cold and distant and she sat very straight. But how lucky she had said "sir"!

"Hanne, Count af Rosenborg," she said, as coldly as she could.

"Good, Mistress Hanne." The man was easy and amiable, and the light from the stove glowed and winked in the buttons of his doublet. "It is certain we will meet again. I am at Kronborg myself, in attendance on the King. This is my hunting lodge." He got up and leaned an elbow on the warm top of the stove. Hanne thought of the icy cold and the clouds of whirling snow beyond the windows.

"There is not much to hunt just now, Count Andreas," she said politely.

"No." Suddenly his easy air was gone, and his eyes on her were sharp and dark. "No. There is not much to hunt just now."

There was a long moment of silence, and now Hanne felt confused and touched by a thread of fear she did not understand. Then the silence broke.

"Andreas!" Loud and cheerful, a man's voice shouted from the shadows of the room beyond and there was a thud of boots across the polished floor.

The man by the stove moved quickly and cried out, but he was not soon enough. Another man was in the room, snow still crusted on his cloak, running into pools around his boots, and falling in lumps from the cap he pulled from his wet hair. He was taller than the Count and very fair, and his clothes were rough and dark. Beside him was a boy.

Hanne looked at him around the corner of her carved chair and then looked again and turned back in amazement to the Count who had halted, his face black with anger, half across the room. The boy was about her own age and his clothes

were poor and rough like those of the man beside him. She studied his dark pleasant face, the snow-wet hair curling to his shoulders, his brisk and amiable air, and saw that he strongly resembled the man who had sat with her this last half hour beside the stove. In silence she stared from one dark face to the other.

"Andreas," shouted the man in the archway again, and his fair cheerful face was full of triumph. "Andreas! It is all here! Mother of God, what a night and what a journey! But it is all here!"

There was a long moment of silence in the room with no sound but the snow hissing down into the stove and the deeply drawn breath of anger from the Count Andreas. The bright-eyed boy looked from one man to the other; and, across the shadows, Hanne watched the boy.

Count Andreas controlled himself and stepped forward quietly.

"Lars," he said slowly and deliberately. "If all the cattle are safe, then I am very pleased. But there is no need to tell me of it here and now. It is the steward's business. Now get along and take your boy with you."

Confusion and astonishment chased each other across the face of the man in the arch, until the grinning boy dug him in the ribs and he finally saw the girl, peering round the high-backed chair. He began at once to roll his cap in his hands and mutter his apologies. He had not hoped to get the herd in tonight, he said, but since he had, he wanted to let his master know. He was sorry to have disturbed his master.

Count Andreas waved him away and he bowed himself out, still muttering. The boy moved slowly to follow him, but his eyes were on Hanne, still staring wide-eyed from her chair.

"My herdsman," Count Andreas said easily when they were gone. "He is a little simple and gets overanxious about his cattle. Now I will see if you may go to bed. They have been warming a bedchamber for you. I wish you good night, Mistress Hanne." With a faint smile he was gone into the shadows after the others.

Left alone, Hanne stared into the red glow of the stove and tried to understand a herdsman who burst into his master's house and called him by his given name; and had a boy to help him who wore the same face as his master.

After a time, a woman came to take her to her bed, and as they passed through the dark archways of the house, she could hear angry voices in the distance.

CHAPTER THREE

Her father smiled his vague kind smile when she told him she wished to be his housekeeper and, at his expression, Hanne's long face took on its affronted flush.

"No, my daughter," he said, and gathered up a roll of charts and plans from the table. His thin clever face so like her own was amused as he looked with absent affection at the tall grave girl whom he had last seen as a little child. "I have no need of a housekeeper. The castle servants bring my meals when I have time to eat them, and Hans and Georg have care of all the rest. There will be a serving woman for you. No, Hanne, you will enjoy yourself with the other children and share their tutors and their lessons. I wanted you to come here so that you might have a livelier life than you have had in that lonely house with your Aunt Elena. You should enjoy it here, and grow up more happily. The children here always seem to me to have much to do."

He turned away from the deep window, where the snow-light washed the white walls with a brilliance that did not touch the deep shadows of the room. Beyond the cobbled courtyard and the bastion wall, the sea was gray and harsh across the Sound to Sweden. His mind was on his work. When he took down the bastion wall in the spring to build the new East Wing, he must keep the building low so as not to lose the sea view to these west windows.

Hanne watched him, her teeth sharp on her lower lip. He had scarcely thought of what she said and had looked at her no more than he had ever done. He still treated her as a child, and she did not want to be again among a crowd of children. They would only laugh at her and call her a prig. They always did. Sick disappointment filled her. Could she face this strange new world and remain only Hanne, who, however hard she tried to be grown-up and good, could never be good enough to make her father notice her.

"Come," her father said now. The last snowlight had left the room, and he spoke from the shadows by the glowing stove. "Get your cloak and I'll take you to see the great new Hall. It is nearly finished. You are rested now from that dreadful journey? Thank Providence you are safe. Come then, or it will be dark."

She went to find her cloak, struggling with a surge of shyness that made her want to cry out and refuse to venture into this strange unfamiliar world. She was still tired and frightened by the nightmare of the snow. In her sleeping chamber she snatched her cloak from the press. The room was high and narrow and the icy light did no more than linger round the windows. Shadows were thick on the coffined ceiling and around the huge curtained bed, and the air was dark and bitter. When she got back to her father, by the warm friendly stove, her heart was banging with fear and loneliness. But the face she turned to him was quiet and untroubled. With her head held high, she followed him down the shadowy stairs and out into the cobbled courtyard.

Even in the bitter weather, Kronborg rang with the frenzy of its building. The castle now enclosed three sides of an immense court and its pale stone walls shut out the winter sky, although the last cold evening light was held in the glinting copper of the new roof. Hanne and her father picked their way across the court and through piles of timber and great frosted blocks of red Scanian sandstone; carved balustrades ready to crown the rampart walls and the round stone balls on which Master van Maebergen would balance the fine points of his wooden spires. Hanne proceeded quietly in her composed fashion, but kept looking anxiously around her to try and see everything at once and make the right comments to her father. She stared from the spark-shot darkness of the forge in the corner to the immense black-mouthed cannon that crowned the rampart between her and the sea.

"Father! For what are the great guns?"

Her shin barked sharply on a balk of timber and she almost fell. She steadied herself and the voice that laughed beside her was not her father's.

"For what are the great guns?" it mocked. "What a little ignoramus you are! And clumsy too. Falling over everything!"

Her skirts had caught in the timber. Angrily she tried to pull them free, then staggered as the cloth ripped. She turned toward the voice, only to stop dead with her mouth open and the folds of her mantle gathered in her hands. Leaning over a pile of sandstone blocks, and watching her with his easy amiable grin, was the dark boy who, with the herdsman, had burst into the room of Count Andreas that night of the fearful journey. Now the cloak around his shoulders was rich and red and his curls fell sleek above fine points of lace below a velvet cap. But the handsome lively face of the boy was still the image of Count Andreas. Before she could collect herself, he spoke again.

"The cannon, my poor simple wench, are to enforce the

dues. The Sound dues," he added, noting her bewildered face. "Did you not know? By my soul, what ignorance. His Majesty of Denmark claims dues from all ships that pass below these walls through the Sound. Sometimes they are not willing—hence the cannon. All ships, that is, except the Swedes." His face darkened and the grin left it. "They have won by war the right to pay no dues."

Hanne found her voice.

"Who *are* you?" she asked him, rubbing at her sore shin, too hurt and angry to be shy. "Who *are* you?"

The boy eased himself from behind the blocks and sauntered round to her. His suit was black, and the buckles of his square-toed shoes winked with diamonds in the failing light.

"Ah-ha," he said, and his dark face gleamed with mischief. "Who am I? Who indeed? I know who you are. You are the daughter of our good Master Maebergen here." He gestured back to where her father had paused to speak with two of his workmen. He looked her up and down then; her plain tidy kirtle and the neat hair tucked so smooth under her little cap. "The daughter of the most famous architect in Flanders—and a prig to boot, unless I am mistaken." There was a sudden wilful cruelty in his voice.

Unwonted temper flared in Hanne, and color glowed in her pale cheeks. "I am not a prig," she hissed. "Nor am I ashamed to say *who* I am. I am my father's daughter, here or anywhere else I go. What were you doing in the hunting lodge of Count Andreas on the first night of the snow, dressed as a peasant? Or are you a peasant really, and all this is a disguise?" She flapped a furious hand at his black and crimson finery. " 'Tis true you have a peasant's manners!"

The boy had grown quiet as she spoke, and now he looked at her and raised indifferent eyebrows, kicking at a piece of broken mortar with the toe of his jeweled shoe. For a moment he did not answer and they stood in silence, looking at each other in the cold gathering shadows. From the forge in the corner, the clang of the hammer seemed edged with the sharpness of the frost and men's voices were clear like bells.

"I?" he said then, and his dark eyes slid away from hers. "I have not been in the hunting lodge of the Count Andreas these many months. And disguised as a peasant?" Now he was all formality. "I am afraid, Mistress van Maebergen, you have been mistaken. You have seen some other boy." He turned and gave a small formal bow to her father who had come up to them. "Master van Maebergen," he said politely, and turned and vanished between the piles of stone.

"Hanne. The light is going. We must get on or you will see nothing this evening."

Hanne did not look at him, but stared in amazement at the spot where the boy had disappeared.

"Father! Who was that boy?" Her voice was baffled.

"That boy?" Her father was already moving away, and she scrambled after him, terrified that she might not hear. "That is Carl Adam, the son of Count Andreas who brought you safely yesterday to Kronborg. He is very like his father, is he not? And a great favorite about the court. A pleasing boy, well-mannered," he ended vaguely.

His eyes moved upward to the stem of a tall tower that was still shrouded in heavy scaffolds, and his mind was already elsewhere. He did not notice that Hanne gave him no answer. Thinking furiously, she followed him in silence to the door which opened into the base of the slender tower. She did not even lift her eyes to the tower itself, climbing to the dark winter sky above the pale fresh stone of the newly built South Wing. Her mind was too busy.

If that was the son of Count Andreas, why did he pretend to be a herdsman's boy in his own house? And why did he deny that he was ever there at all? Were there two of him? Had he a twin brother? But then, a twin must also be the son of Count Andreas and should not behave like a young herdsman either.

Confused and bewildered, Hanne paused in the darkness and groped for the lowest step of the narrow spiral stair. Each step was so perfect that it seemed to lift with its own strength up out of the darkness to the torchlight glowing above her on the rising walls. At the top of the stairs she followed her father through the opening for a door.

The Hall before her was vast beyond her wildest dream. Even in its piled, confused, and unfinished state it was so beautiful that she stood still and absolutely silent, marveling that she had a father who could raise such beauty from the heaps of wood and stone that lay snow-encrusted in the courtyard.

It was very, very long, but not high. The wall across from her held a row of great square-paned windows, deep set in the immense thickness of the walls and filling the whole Hall with the strange blue-green of snowlight over a winter sea. The Hall was full of people; humming with the chatter of carpenters, painters, plasterers; littered with work benches; warmed by whole tree trunks burning in vast grates at either end, and glowing braziers set along its length. Half the low ceiling was still bare and raftered, the other half intricately carved and glorious with the fresh color of painted panels picked out with gold. Even as she watched, four careful workmen eased another panel into place. Her father came back and stood beside her. "You like it, my daughter? It is called the Knights' Hall."

Hanne had not yet found words. He did not wait for an answer.

"Master Kneiper of Holland has been bidden to weave the tapestries for the walls. It will be very splendid."

Almost at once he was gone again, and Hanne looked after him unhappily. She had been summoning so many things to say; clever things to make him see that she really tried to understand his work. But he threw her a vague word and was gone, and all her good clever phrases went unsaid. She moved out into the middle of the room. The great windows were on both sides of it, the light from the two long perfect rows meeting in a flood in the middle of the pale checkered floor below the gilded ceiling. No one paid her any attention, and she walked shyly through the bustle of workmen, feeling the slip of the smooth marble underneath her shoes and lifting her head to pick out each detail of the ceiling.

A hand grasped her arm and pulled her to one side.

"Have care! You will fall again. Do you never watch where you are going?"

She did not need to look to know the teasing voice, and she shook the hand off her arm irritably. She had no shyness with this boy. He angered her too much.

"I know well where I am going. And I always look!"

"Well, look behind you now, then!"

She jumped just in time to avoid one of the great carved panels of the ceiling, carried by two men. Scrambling out of their way, she knocked a table, and a chisel clattered to the floor. Carl Adam leaped to catch a falling pot of paint. He was doubled up with laughter.

"I am glad you do look," he cried, "for Heaven keep us from what would happen if you didn't. Come over here, safely out of the way, before there is more harm. Your father does not mind us children coming here to look, but only if we behave as if we are not here at all. A little more of this, and he will put you out."

Smarting with shame and anger, she longed to contradict him, but she knew that it was true. Even in the great workshop at home, she might only come and see his models if she was quiet and orderly and did not touch. Sourly she followed the boy into one of the alcoves of the great windows, and pressed her face against the glass so that she need not look at him. Far below her lay the cold gray sea, and, lights pricked out beyond the water on the coast of Sweden. Already, so early in the year, loose ice floated in the unfriendly water and the vast wide sky was filled with bitter light that seemed to struggle against darkness. She shivered and forgot her anger.

"This strange light," she said. "I do not like it. Over the sea the dusk is almost white."

"Oh, no." He was quite ready to be friendly now. "That is only the snowlight. The white twilight comes in summer. Did you not know? Dusk is long and strange and the light on the sea is white. My father tells me that farther north the night does not fall at all; that in summer the daylight stays all the hours through, and then in winter, there is no day."

Hanne turned from the window and looked at him in disbelief. No night? No day? She felt sure that it was nonsense. And how would his father, in waiting on the King, come to know these things?

"Your father?" she said, curiosity getting the better of her manners. "How does he know these things?"

To her surprise, the boy was disturbed. For a moment his self-confidence left him and he looked away from her, fiddling with the latches on the window.

"Why shouldn't he?" he answered slowly. "He has sailed when he was younger. Over all the northern seas."

They looked at each other then for a long moment, as though meeting each other for the first time; and outside the window the light grew purple over the wide sea.

"You have no mother?" he asked suddenly.

"No. She died when I was born."

"Mine also." As he spoke, they looked at each other again, sharing a sudden sense of loss, although they did not know what they had lost.

"Come." Carl Adam flung away from the window. "Your father is busy. We will go up the Trumpeters' Tower. He does not truly like us to go alone, but he's too busy to notice. Come."

Hanne held back. Her shyness had returned a hundred fold after that brief moment of confidence.

"No." She drew back into the window. "It is not right, if my father——"

The boy's face had lost its friendliness. He shrugged his crimson-clad shoulders and the light of a new-lit torch winked and glittered in his silver brooch.

"I knew it," he said derisively. "I knew you were a prig. It shows. Ah well—I will go alone."

Hanne was before him. "Where is it?" Her long mouth was tight.

"How little you know of your father's castle!"

"I have but been here a day," she snapped.

He looked at her and went on more quietly, "It is this tower—the one you and your father just climbed. It faces the main gate of the castle, and there is to be a gallery at the very top, where the trumpeters can blow a fanfare for the King or his guests as they ride in. Be careful. The tower is not finished."

Hanne did not understand herself. Never before would she have given the smallest thought to any act that might displease her father. Now here she was doing something forbidden because she could not bear this boy to call her prig. She had been called it often before, and had only put up her nose and struggled to be even better. This time she had to prove the name wrong.

The stairs above the level of the hall were dark, and she groped her way up behind the boy. As the darkening sky showed over their heads, the boy leaned down and gave her a hand.

"You will be quite safe. There is a wooden railing, so you cannot fall."

He pulled her out on to the top of the half-finished tower, and after one glance, Hanne closed her eyes and groped blindly for the rail. Thankfully, she felt it cold and rough under her hands, and slowly she opened her eyes again, waiting for the dark sea and the white snow-covered land to cease their whirling and settle back where they belonged.

"Are you all right?" she heard the boy say.

Desperately she answered, "Yes." And in a while she was. It was almost night now, and she looked down on the piled confusion of the courtyard crossed and recrossed with flickering lights; over to the old buildings in their shadowed masses, and to the great fortified wall toward the sea, where her father would be building in the spring. While she watched, the small glow of candles was kindled in the rows of windows as servants moved through the chambers with a taper, and the warm evening castle sprang to life in the dark stone that had seemed so empty and forbidding. As the cold wind whipped and tore at her skirts and snatched her hair from its bands beneath her cap, a sudden new excitement took her; to be so high and secret with the stars shining in the cold close sky and the dark sea stretching unseen along the edges of the snow-covered land. Beyond the shadows of the forest, the lights winked from a small town. It must be Elsinore. She searched the flat snow wastes for other lights, other people, but suddenly Carl Adam nudged her, and spoke urgently.

"See who comes," he said. "See who comes."

She peered down, her fear of the height forgotten.

A blaze of torchlight crossed the courtyard from the north side. She could see little but the shapes of men in the red unsteady light.

"Well? Who comes?"

"The King. He loves his new castle, and cannot leave your poor father to work in peace."

"Oh!" She leaned over in her curiosity and the boy grabbed her by the cloak.

"No need to cast yourself as an offering at his feet."

"But which is the King?"

"The dark one in the purple cloak. He is not very tall. See, the light falls on him now."

"Oh, yes." She was a little disappointed in the short dark man in the unimportant-looking cloak. "But see who is with him."

The boy was silent.

"The Count Andreas—your father."

"Yes," he said, and did not move or speak again until the party of men had gone into the tower below them. "Yes," he said again, and eased himself from the rail. "My father." He turned to the dark hole of the stairs. "Come see what they are about," he said.

Darkness had fallen in the Knights' Hall. Torches had been lit along the walls and candles placed in branches on the tables, but they gave light only for the men to clear away their tools and set aside their work. The day was over.

The King stood with Hanne's father, bent over piled plans on a table, the shadows of the candlelight deep in his strong dark face. At his elbow was Count Andreas. Down in the great room the workmen waited in respectful but uneasy silence, and there was quiet save for the hissing of the torches and the occasional falling of a log.

"They could kill him when he comes at this hour," whispered the boy. "They want nothing but to get through the

woods to Elsinore before the darkness grows too thick."

They were not to go early that night.

There was a sudden clatter of boots on the spiral stair, followed by the slow heavy thump of more reluctant feet.

"Master van Maebergen!" The man who burst in was so excited he failed to see the King. "Master van Maebergen!" He threaded his way across the shadowed checkered floor. "Master—the ship you waited for has come! The one with the valuable cargo! Rifled again——! Oh—your Majesty, your pardon. I did not see you in the shadows. I thought Master van Maebergen to be alone. I thought—I did not know——!"

Hanne's father did not speak, helpless to save the man, who bowed and backed away in stuttering confusion, ready to bolt now as fast as he had come. Hanne looked at the boy beside her and saw him watching with a strange still face and wide eyes dark with tension. Something about him held her for a moment, and then she turned back to the thunder of anger from the King.

"What ship?" His dark face was thrust across the candle-light and his shadow sprawled gigantic on the painted ceiling. "What ship, I say? Another taken by this thieving pirate, is it? What is my Navy doing that my ships cannot sail the waters of my country without being ravaged by these brigands! What ship and what valuable cargo?"

His voice grew ominously quiet on the last sentence and, desperately, the poor fellow garbled out the story that would have been far better taken to the King in private, at some mellow time when bad news might come more easily.

"A ship, Majesty, from Jutland, laden with copper for the

facing of the roof and quantities of amber to inlay the doors, and," he swallowed hopelessly and then burst out with the worst of it, "large quantities of gold leaf for the ceilings."

"Gone?" asked the King across the table in the same quiet voice.

"Yes, Majesty. I have the master of the ship himself to tell of it."

The heavy boots of the seaman thumped heavily into the space in the middle of the floor. He pulled off his woolen cap and bowed before his King. He was awkward and uneasy, shaken by the loss of his cargo and now overwhelmed by the grandeur of this mighty shadowed room and frightened by the angry face across the table.

"I could not help it, Majesty," he blurted out. "They were on us in the dark without a sound. The first evening of the snow, it was. We had turned the northern point of Zeeland, by that fishing village where the watch fire burns, and we were running for Kronborg through the snow. She edged up beside us like a phantom, and they were aboard before we could cry out! Two to one, they were, and three of my good fellows died before they took us over. A whole mob they had to transfer the cargo, and then they cut us loose and vanished in the snow. They could have gone anywhere."

"And you?"

"I tried to follow, Sir, and searched the coast. It is a mass of small bays and coves along there to the north. All the next day I searched. That is why I am overdue. I found nothing. No ship. No cargo. Nothing."

He twirled his blue cap in his fingers and looked anxiously at the King.

The answer was the crash of the King's fist on the table. The plans scattered and the candles leaped in their sockets, splashing the hot wax on his hands. He snatched them back and clapped them together with the sudden pain.

"I will have it stopped," he roared. "Five years ago we rolled their heads here in the marketplace, and I thought my seas were clear! This is one, they tell me. One audacious thief! Well, this head will roll, too, until I and my people can sail our seas in peace. *Every* pirate. It must *stop*."

At each end of the long Hall the huge fires were scarlet in the darkness, and among the watching crowd the braziers glowed. The King eased himself up from the table and, without a further glance to anyone, he turned towards the door. Hanne, watching, saw Count Andreas follow him and, across the shadows, his eyes met those of his son. But she could not read their look.

CHAPTER FOUR

The bitter Danish winter dragged its way through the long dark months. Through the archways of the castle the icy winds moaned and whistled off the northern seas. The craftsmen blew on their numbed fingers and dragged their tables closer to the fires. In the courtyard the fair fresh stone of Master van Maebergen made a strange patchwork of the ancient buildings, and the new red sandstone facing to the sea already looked old and faded against the spotless capping of the tedious months of snow.

There were a score or more children in the castle; sons and daughters of the nobles-in-waiting on the King, or of officers in charge of the garrison. Like most of the people of their cold windswept land, they were cheerful and friendly, and would have taken Hanne at once into their little company. They watched her sedate and stilted ways with surprised dark eyes and then laughed and paid little heed. Gradually she began to lose her shyness and move into the young life of these children who took her so for granted. Only Carl Adam could still catch her eye and bring unwilling pinkness to her cheeks as she hesitated on the brink of some boisterous game along the windswept ramparts; or stood back in the shadows to watch the other children on informal evenings when the King chose to dine with all his household in the old dining hall above the kitchens.

When the tables had been cleared he would lean back benevolently in his carved chair. "The King is not at home," he would cry, and then his household could relax. With all the others, he would smile and clap for the dancing children, until they were sent off to their beds along the icy passages, leaving the warm candlelight and the lilting music to their parents.

"You are happy in Kronborg, my Hanne?"

Her father paused beside her one day in the new Hall, where the whole ceiling now glowed in matchless color, and light flooded the checkered floor, pouring in through the great windows off a sea that was darkening with the first living blue of spring.

"Yes, Father, very happy." She looked at him hopefully, waiting for him to ask more. She longed to loose the imprisoned words and tell him how she had grown to love the winter castle, like a fortress against cold and danger; in the firelight and candlelight with the changing colors of the sea below its windows; and now, with the first pale sunshine lying in pools across the polished floors.

She shot a shy glance at him, but he was unrolling a parchment and did not seem to have heard her answer. She said no more, but turned to the window and, for a moment, struggled to hold back the sudden tears.

She tried so hard to please him, to be grown-up and useful, but he never seemed to notice. If he found her fair head bent above the inkstains on his doublet, he would look at her in vague surprise and ask her why she did not let the serving wenches clean his clothes.

While the other children raced along the ramparts, she pored over the great books on architecture that lay about his room, and then tried to speak to him of all she read. Her father only smiled at her with the same vague amusement he had given to the dancing bear that had gamboled in the courtyard at the Feast of Yul.

Now, when she moved away, he lifted his head and looked at her for a moment, the pale sun catching the gray hair above his ears and turning it to silver. He thought of her more than she knew, and wondered why she was not more like other children. So pale, she was, and colorless. Was it wrong to feel that his daughter should sometimes give a little *trouble?* She seemed so much less quick to laugh than all the other boisterous children who plagued his workmen round the buildings. Her tutors praised her, her music teacher spoke of her great talent, her sewing mistress cried out in delight at her embroidery and vowed she had her father's clever fingers. Master van Maebergen sighed. He loved to have her near him, was proud of all her gifts, but he was too busy, always too busy, to give her more than a moment's thought.

"Good, my daughter, good," he answered now. It must suffice that she was content, and that pediment above the door might prove a little difficult to set. He must watch the men. Already he was moving away, tall and thin and abstracted, his green doublet taking the sudden color that belonged to everything on this first bright day.

Hanne stood a moment looking after him, and then turned back and looked across the racing Sound, wild with the winds of spring that were tossing the ships that lay below the castle walls. She shrugged and drifted off along the Hall. She was due at her music lesson in the dark small room at the bottom of the old tower, sheltered from the sun and the white sea light by the height of the rampart wall outside. She threw a restless look towards the tumbling sea, and threaded her fingers through the ribbons of her lute. What was wrong with her?

All the years of Aunt Elena's training were not for nothing. She took her eyes from the water, straightened her shoulders, and made dutifully for the old stairs in the corner of the Hall.

"Always on time! Such a good pupil!"

She avoided Carl Adam as much as she could. She had seen no more that was strange, yet her mind kept coming back to the mystery of her first days at Kronborg. And he made her uncomfortable. He did not jeer at her. He teased and asked her to laugh at herself. She could not. She stopped now, as easily offended as ever, cheeks pink and ready to defend herself against the bright-eyed boy who sat in the deep window at the bottom of the stairs, swinging his long legs in yellow hose and biting happily at a length of sausage.

"Piece?" he asked amiably, before she could speak.

"No! And I am not always first," she added unwisely. "You are here before me."

"Ah—but not inside. Nor likely to go. It is too good a day. I am off to the forest with my father, to seek the prospects of a hunt within a week or two." He looked again at his piece of sausage, bright red skin between his fingers, and his soft leather jerkin creaked a little in the silence as he moved. "Don't know what's wrong with sausage," he added. "Excellent. The cook gave it to me to get rid of me." He raised his teasing eyebrows and held it out again.

"*No!*" How could he not see that she was not the kind of girl to gnaw a length of sausage! She whirled away, forgetting she was on the last step of the stairs. Tangled skirts caught her ankles and she almost fell, tossing the lute across the stone floor. Tears were hot against her eyes. How was it that this boy could *always* make her seem stupid! Scarlet with shame and anger, she took the lute he had leaped to pick up. He bowed as he gave it to her and twanged a couple of discords on the strings.

"No sausage," he said firmly, and she could not tell if he were laughing. "But you will come on the hunt when we arrange it? Surely? It will be better, I tell you, than tittupping with your master round the riding school in Antwerp. I have seen you riding since the snow melted and I tell you, you ride well for a girl. Very well," he added kindly.

She felt a faint color that was, for once, not anger stain her cheeks.

"I—I would like to hunt." She was embarrassed by his praise, and by the dark blue eyes that always watched her with a strange expression when they were not teasing. "But —my father cannot spare the time, I am sure."

"Your father? What of him? I have never seen him on a horse. All the Court will be a-hunting. To my father's lodge. It makes no matter if your father is not there. Take his man Georg. And I will care for you, too," he added handsomely.

Hanne's long eyes were wide and nervous.

"It would not be proper. It would not be right. Without my father I—no, I couldn't come."

"It would not be proper. It would not be right!" Sudden cruelty was in his voice again as he mimicked her. "Do you never get tired of doing always what is right?"

He left her then, cramming the last of his sausage into his mouth, his face dark with disgust. The heavy oak door slammed behind him and Hanne stared after him; then carefully smoothed the ribbons of the lute and straightened her wide skirts. Calm and quiet again, she went in to her lesson. Of course it would not be proper!

Yet two evenings later, her father lifted his tired face from his heaped table, and looked at her across the candlelight.

"Hanne, daughter—I am glad you are going on the hunt. It will be an outing for you. I fear I am too busy to give you much pleasure."

"I? Going on the hunt?"

"Yes—why did you not ask yourself? I told Carl Adam that you surely could, if Georg escorted you. He is a pleasing boy, that son of Count Andreas."

Hanne laid her embroidery in her lap and the small affectionate smile that touched his lips did not escape her. *Everybody* loved this irritating boy. Her father *saw* Carl Adam, even if he did not see her. What was wrong with her? Was she not real? She bit back a sudden flare of jealousy and managed with an effort to smile and thank him for giving his permission.

When the day came for the hunt, she could not hold to her irritation. She was pale with nervousness at finding herself alone among the crowd of ladies in their bright full-skirted habits and their nodding plumes. She could see no other girls; only Carl Adam in the middle of a group of boys. Wearing a sober suit of forest green, he was petting the pale arching neck of his Norwegian horse. She clung close to

Georg as they gathered in the stable yard below the bastions and waited for the King, but her shyness was lost when, with a hollow clatter, they crossed the drawbridge over the still waters of the moat and headed over the flat springtime fields beside the sea, toward the dark forest that lay close below the walls of Kronborg.

It was the first hunt of the season to replenish the castle larders, which had been emptied of fresh meat through the long snowbound winter. Across the young shining grass the wind blew fresh and soft, and below the fields the sands were yellow against the new blue of the sea. Every now and then the air was heavy with the beat of great white wings as the storks circled and searched, looking for their springtime homes on the tall red chimneys of Elsinore. Everywhere, people lifted their heads and smiled at the great birds, for good fortune came with them and the town would prosper where they built their nests.

Hanne's reins grew slack upon her horse's neck as she stared all round her in delight. Winter had closed her in the shelter of the castle and although she had walked on the bastion walls above the sea, this was her first real sight of this new country with its soft yet brilliant colors, and some strange enchantment in its clear air.

Now the flying color of the hunt was fast and furious through the long glades of the forest; pursuing first one quarry and then another. The baying of hounds and the blaring of horns flushed the birds in startled flocks from the dark pine trees and sent the small animals flying panic-stricken to their holes.

By midday the bags grew heavy at the servants' saddles

and they all gathered for their meal at the hunting lodge of Count Andreas.

"It looks a thought different, Mistress Hanne, from when last we saw it." Georg spoke from behind her as they jogged along the ride between the spreading fingers of the pines, touched at their tips with the tender green of the young season. Hanne turned to him, her eyes bright and her pale cheeks flushed with the speed and pleasure of her morning's ride.

"I like it better thus, Georg!"

Daylight showed the lodge to be a long low house of a single story, set on a slight grass-grown rise in the very heart of the forest and crowned with the pale amber of an ancient thatch. Its walls were painted a rich dark red, and beside the front door was the wide window from which light had beckoned them through the torn whirling of the snow.

Hanne gave her reins to Georg and slipped from her saddle, her eyes on the house and her mind on the stormy night she had been there. Would she see anything more today? All winter, Carl Adam had seemed exactly what he was: the son of Count Andreas, page to his father on all formal days and, to her, the most irritating tease in the castle.

The lodge was not large, and the hunting party filled it. She threaded her way through the warm, chattering crowd, flushed and hungry from their long morning; chewing on roast goose and arguing the day's sport. The rooms, as she faintly remembered, had no doors. One dark-paneled chamber opened straight through an archway to the next, so that the house was really one vast room. It did not take her long to worm her way into the room where she had been before.

She ran a finger over the remembered tiles around the stove and looked across at the archway where the fair-haired man and the boy had stood, crusted and dripping with snow. She felt bewildered. The memory had the strange feeling of a dream, and was easy to disbelieve. But she knew it to be true. She turned suddenly with a sense that she was being watched.

Across the room, as though they were alone, and the crowded floor between them empty, Carl Adam stood as still as she, a half-eaten meat pie in his hands and his eyes as steady on her as if he read her thoughts. At once, when she looked at him, he smiled and seized another pie from a table, edging his way across to her among the press of people.

"You do not eat, Mistress Hanne," he said. "And it is not sausage!" Lies or no lies, mystery or no mystery, Hanne had only to look at the food to know that she was starving. But she watched him across the top of her fresh ham pie as it crumbled on her chin. She brushed the crumbs aside and swallowed the mouthful whole, afraid that he would go.

"You *were* here!" How could he deny it now that they stood in the same room?

"I was where?"

"Here!" Hanne almost stamped. "Here in this room on the first night of the snow. With a fair-haired man who called Count Andreas by his given name. You stood over there, in that arch!" How could he deny it?

For a long moment he looked at her and the girl saw suddenly that his eyes were frightened. She was gentle and pity struck her quickly, but before she could speak he had recovered.

"I am afraid, Mistress Hanne, you must be having girlish dreams! And you must always do what is right, you know," he went on mockingly. "And it is not right to tell lies. Not right at all." He looked back as he moved off. "Also, you have crumbs on your chin!"

Yet, later in the day, the run of the hunt threw them together and, through the pale declining afternoon, they rode side by side, taking pleasure in each other's horsemanship. The forest here was open, the huge pine trees spaced so that the fading sun struck through them in a haze of tender green. In the spaces at their feet, tiny saplings pointed towards the sky and the soft grass was starred and spangled with the first small flowers of spring. The cool blue shadows of the early dusk were gathering beneath the trees when, together, the boy and girl crashed into an open ride, a little to one side of the hunt.

The ride stretched away before them; green and empty and silent and hazed with gold from the last of the sun. Flushed and panting they looked at each other for one brief second; then they laughed and steadied their horses.

"Off!" cried the boy, and their flying hooves were silent on the turf. The dark trees rushed past them and the flaring horns grew faint in the distance. It was the girl who at last called a halt, shouting to the boy and reining in her horse. He slowed and circled and came back to her, thinking her to be quite another girl, with her scarlet cheeks and wide shining eyes.

"Georg will kill me, so to tire the horse," she gasped. "But that was good. Good!"

"I said you did not ride too badly for a girl."

This time she was not angry. She shifted a little in her saddle.

"I think I have loosed a girth. And I have lost Georg. Will you tighten it for me?"

He opened his mouth to answer but, at that moment, a little down the ride, there was a soft rustle in the trees and a young deer, separated from its mother by the hunt, leaped into the open and stood a moment, trembling on its pale delicate legs and with its soft nose lifted to the strange noises and the smell of danger.

"Young venison!" Carl Adam shouted in delight. The deer was off and he after it, crashing into the dark trees where the animal had vanished.

Hanne pursed her lips and waited. Soon she grew a little anxious, watching the pale sunlight fade along the ride and the shadows come down with a blue chill that still held the last traces of the winter. In the end she slipped off and tightened up her girth herself, struggling awkwardly and angrily with her full skirts when she had to mount again alone. When at last she had heaved herself into the saddle, she looked in despair up and down the long shadowed ride where darkness crept in from the trees. The last sounds of the hunt had faded into silence and she had no idea where she was. This whole escapade would gain her a good scolding from Georg even if he did not tell her father. But the darkness was growing and she shivered with cold and the first touch of fear. There is the sun setting, she told herself firmly, so that must be the west. The forests where we hunt are to the north of Kronborg, so if I ride towards the south, I cannot go far wrong. And a ride as wide and straight at this was surely made by man. This must lead somewhere.

Resolutely, she argued with herself and trotted firmly and steadily to the south, keeping her eyes from the thick darkness that was gathering beneath the trees, even though the sky above the ride was still clear with lingering light and patched with the first stars. So soon that she almost laughed at her fears, a ride which opened to her left led to an open rise of land, crowned, in the shadowy distance, with the unmistakable long dark bulk of the hunting lodge. On this side of it, the gentle slope was covered with a huddle of outhouses whose white walls stood out in the spring dusk.

She turned toward them thankfully. Her pleasure in the thought of company and safety was mixed with the fear of Georg's tongue, when he discovered that one of his horses had been maltreated. If only he didn't stop her going out again. She never had trouble being good, except when she was with Carl Adam. But she must not blame him. He had not *made* her race. She could have said no.

Busy with her conscience, she was too late to stop her horse from stepping on something that lay in the middle of the narrow ride; fluttering a little in the wind and gleaming with a steady brilliance that even the growing darkness could not dim. She did not see it until the hoof went down, and then she jerked at the astonished horse. Amazed, and a little afraid, she slipped from the saddle, looking round her at the crowding trees. Hanging the reins across her arm, she lifted up the horse's hoof and saw that it glittered with dust and broken fragments; the pale unmistakable shimmer of pure gold. She had seen it just before the hoof came down and she had recognized the shape. She had seen many of these by now; the small sheets of leaf gold from which the craftsmen laid their gilding with such care onto the panels of the new ceiling.

Hanne shivered. Count Andreas! The King's friend. It was not possible. Who could she tell? How could she begin to tell her father what she thought, and what could he do? It would be his death if he were proved wrong. She could not tell Carl Adam because it was his father's house and he had told her cold lies already so that she did not trust him. This was *wickedness*. Her natural righteousness began to assert itself. Somebody should be told, but who?

She sighed and shook her head and bent again to tear fistfuls of the soft young grass and clean the gleaming hoof. Tired and puzzled and a little frightened, she pushed the grass away inside a thick bush. She had enough to explain to Georg already.

But when Georg at last found her, holding her exhausted horse in the crowd before the lodge, he looked once at the young anxious face and did not scold at all.

CHAPTER FIVE

The clear windy days lengthened slowly, and summer brought the strange enchantment of the long white twilights. Every evening when the meal was done, Hanne slipped away to walk along the bastions behind the great cannon that crouched above the Sound. She was fascinated by this strange unearthly color that chilled the sea and laid its white icy fingers along the land, bleaching the rocks below the castle and sharpening the darkness of the forest so that every pointed pine seemed separate against the sky.

"I told you that in summer the twilight would be white."

Carl Adam had come up behind her where she sat in her favorite place in all the castle since the summer days had come; on the heights of the flag battery. Here she was watched by the indulgent sailor whose duty lay in answering the salutes of shipping, dipping the white and scarlet flag that took such brilliant color in the sharp light. She loved to sit here, peering dangerously down at the far grass below her where it withered and grew sparse in the sand that edged the tideless sea. Sweden seemed a hand's breadth away, and the great black tower of Karna looked harmless as a pasteboard toy. Hanne knew it bristled with cannon as large and fearsome as the row of muzzles that yawned along the bastion walls of Kronborg. Between them lay the ships, idle in the quiet evening on the bleached and glittering sea. They rocked gently while their captains rowed ashore to pay the dues and the water fell white as ice from the small splash of their oars.

"It is beautiful, is it not, our Denmark?"

The boy leaned beside her on the bastion wall and his eyes roamed over the sea. Hanne's soft heart warmed to his simple pride in his country. He was quiet this evening, not in his usual teasing mood; his face serious and his eyes on the passing ships. In this tranquil moment she longed to ask all the questions that had troubled her through the long spring days. But, even as she opened her mouth to speak, he turned himself to yawn and stretch. He had taken off his jerkin and his ruff stuck out, crumpled, from the pocket of his breeches. His throat was brown under his open shirt, as though in these summer days his ruff was more often in his pocket than on his neck. She had seen him very little lately; only in passing, riding out with a crowd of other boys, a falcon hooded on his bright wrist and the plumes waving from his velvet cap. Or rushing through the gateway of the castle as the great bell rang for noon, his shirt wet and his hair plastered from the sea, he would roll his eyes at her in pantomime of panic that he would not be ready to wait on his father at the midday meal.

"I am going for a sail," he said now. "The only place for an evening such as this is on the sea. Were you not so full of virtues, I would take you with me. But you, no doubt, would say that you are not allowed."

Hanne closed her mouth. What a waste of time to think of talking to him. She would only have been told more lies. Her lips tightened and her face returned to its habitual primness.

"Of course. If I am not allowed then, I must not go."

"I must not go," he mimicked. "Do you never do anything because you *want* to, and take the punishment if you are caught, whether it be right or wrong?" His young face was almost angry and she felt feeble and foolish and threatened with imminent tears. This boy was brought up at Court, by a handsome worldly father. How to tell him of her closed life in the tall red house in Antwerp, under the rigid rule of prayers and duty that was all Aunt Elena knew. These last four years she had been quite alone with her aunt, and there was never any thought of what she might *want* to do. Duty ordered a certain time to do a certain thing, and it was done. And always she, herself, must struggle to be good, to be worthy of her father, but now she looked at the boy's contemptuous eyes and felt the old inadequacy creep over her. This time she had not even anger to protect her from it.

"I don't know," she said feebly.

"Well, do know, girl. Why should you not sail with me?"

"I—I think my father would say it isn't safe. He has never allowed me." She did not add that she had never asked.

"Never allowed you! There you are again! And not safe!" He turned and looked at her in the weird sharpened light, and his dark eyes were outraged. "And I my father's son."

Some irritation with her had been driving him, but now he was embarrassed and furious with himself, as though he would snatch back the words. Hanne forgot herself at once, remembering that this was the second time he had suggested that his father had been a sailor. Yet she had learned that Count Andreas had been a soldier through all the long Swedish wars and that he had come to the King's notice and gained favor by his valor on the battlefield. He had never been a sailor. They looked at each other for a silent moment of speculation and then he shrugged it off.

"I told you he sailed all the northern seas when he was young."

The boy slipped off the wall beside her and as he heaved his jerkin over his shoulder, his face looked bored. Hanne knew this look well. She had seen it so often on the faces of children who had tried to draw her into mischief and met her prim refusal.

"I'm going." The gravel was noisy under his firm disgusted tread.

"And I!" she cried suddenly after him. Sick excitement shook her along with a tremulous bravado. Why not? She had done all she could to be the best in everything. And did her father see? Now she would be bad. This was bad; much worse than running up the tower, or riding a horse to exhaustion.

Carl Adam turned and his eyes were wide and ready to mock; but when he saw her nervous determined face, he changed.

"You will like it," he said, and his face was suddenly kind.

Hanne looked up guiltily at the circular windows of the Queen's apartments as they trotted down the slope to the main gate. The gentle German-born Queen Sophia had been very gracious to her, sensing the deep shyness of the quiet Flemish girl among the boisterous Danes. Hanne would not like now to be seen scampering down the ramparts with a boy in an unbuttoned shirt, his ruff hanging from his pocket and his jerkin tossed across his shoulder. She put her head down, ran a little faster, and hoped she was not seen.

Even in her ignorance, Hanne could feel that Carl Adam

handled his little boat with skill and confidence. As they drew out into the lifting twilight sea, fear and guilt fell away from her and she looked back in delight at her father's rose-red castle. It rose like a fairy fortress from the water with the last of the sunlight blazing gold from the copper roof. The sea opened wide and limitless to the north beyond the narrow Sound, and all the sky was filled with a deepening ghostly light that seemed to be blown across the surface of the sea, bleaching the water and falling strangely and unearthly on the faces of the girl and boy.

With the skiff bucking to the evening wind, excitement took Hanne like a caught breath. Her linen cap was snatched and flung aside and she laughed out loud as the wind took her long fair hair and plastered it across her face. The boy looked at her in amazement.

"You know, Mistress Hanne, it is the first time I have heard you laugh." He smiled at her eagerly. "You like it? I thought you would. These are the white nights on the sea. Darkness barely falls at all."

He looked at her again as the wind lifted her blown hair about her excited cheeks. Once again, as on the day they raced in the forest, it was hard to believe her the same girl who had crept so primly through the castle all the winter, irritating him with her air of remoteness, of self-satisfaction and good behavior. His grin widened and he began to sing, an old Danish song that all the chldren in the castle sang. In a moment Hanne sang too, a happy doubtful smile on her long face, until she muddled the Danish words and threw the song into confusion. The boy shouted with laughter and stopped.

"You have not your father's voice," he cried, for, in his rare moments of ease, Master van Maebergen would sing most sweetly for them all beside the evening fire.

He was astonished when Hanne fell silent at his words and contentment left her face, giving back her usual look of doubt and shyness. She made the first answer she could think of, echoing what was said by everyone a dozen times a day about the remarkable likeness between Count Andreas and his son.

"We cannot," she said defensively, "be all of us as good as our good fathers."

Now it was his turn to look as though he had been hit. They stared at each other in the blue thickening light as the little boat raced across the luminous sea. Each had hurt the other, touched a sore place they did not understand. They did not understand, but suddenly they were better friends.

"Carl Adam," she said, and called him by his name. "Should we not turn for home?"

But the boy no longer heeded her. He stared fixedly into the distant blackness of the pinewoods on the shore, and then he turned and stared out across the sea. Hanne watched for a moment and then, when he looked back to the shore, she turned to follow his gaze. They were opposite a small cove that stretched two sheltering arms into the water, and in the icy light she could clearly see the small beach with low dunes of yellow sand that reached up to the dark spiked shadows of the pinewoods. Now she saw what he was watching. Above the yellow sand, a small light pricked the darkness again and again, and the boy's eyes were half closed upon it, his face tight with concentration.

"What is it?" She pushed back her windblown hair, the better to see the small jerking light.

He didn't answer until it stopped and the woods were a dark fringe again against the western sky. To the north, the watch fire flared suddenly on the highest of the sandy cliffs, to warn ships of the dangerous shoals.

He shrugged. "Someone making signals," he said indifferently, but his eyes were anything but indifferent as they raked the darkening sea.

"You are right, Hanne," he said, and she noticed that he had dropped the "Mistress," just as she had dropped the "Master" a few moments before. "It is time that we were home."

He put the little boat about into the wind, and they lost speed.

"Here," he said. "I will let you steer. It's very simple."

She did not move, spellbound again by the distant beauty of the castle as they turned towards it. Its vast shadowed bulk rose against the southern sky in an evening light so clear that even here the fragile shelter of the scaffolding was plain around the Trumpeters' Tower, crowned at last with its slender spire. One single brilliant star glowed bright blue-green behind it.

"Venus." The boy threw it a glance as she cried out, and named it, but his eyes were on the sea.

"You know about the stars?"

"Yes." He turned back again. "Yes." He opened his mouth to say something more and then looked at her and closed it. "I know all about the stars," was all he said. But the girl, looking at him across the plunging boat, knew he had been going to say that his father had taught him. All the time, his eyes were on the sea.

After a time and in silence, a ship approached behind them; a vessel of some size, making for the Swedish coast. She bore no lights and the few faces showing above her rail were formless in the dusk. Yet when Carl Adam saw her, he called Hanne to the tiller and showed her quickly how to use it, bidding her to steer for the pale brilliance of Venus and the dark spires of Kronborg. Over her shoulder she watched the vessel, and saw that she was painted in the colors of the sea, blue and green, and barred with shadowy white. Like a ghost the ship passed, her square sails giving to the wind.

Standing at the mast of the little boat, Carl Adam watched with fixed intensity until she was out of sight, swallowed in the dusk.

"What ship is that?" Hanne concentrated now on her star, easing the tiller round before he should notice she had drifted off her course.

"I have no idea." His answer was curt and Hanne had to be content, for his face was closed and dark and she would not ask him more.

By the time they reached his father's slip, he was a boy again, intent on mischief; goading her to follow him.

"The main gate will be shut, you know," he told her cheerfully as he tied the painter to its ring. "We are later than I meant to be."

Hanne looked up above her, and now the fairy evening castle of Kronborg was a black monstrous mass of stone, fringed with the fearsome mouths of cannon. Only a small pale light here and there showed that anything as frail as man might live in it.

"The drawbridge will be up too," he went on happily.

She looked at him in real alarm. "How then do we get in?"

"Well."

They walked across the grass toward the castle ramp, and at their feet small harebells glimmered, holding light when light had left all the world except the northern sky. He looked sideways at her frightened face.

"We could take the great horn that hangs at the outer gate. Have you good wind? It takes a lot to blow it. That would call the Guard. They would be most pleased, and our fathers, no doubt, even more pleased when they were told tomorrow."

Hanne was on the verge of tears. Never had she known her father angry, for she had never given him cause.

"Carl Adam, you are teasing me. How do we get in, I beg you?"

She was frightened now. Through the long winter she had loved the castle, feeling the strength and comfort of the immense walls between her and the snowbound world outside; the dark rooms warm and soft with firelight above the icy seas. Her father's castle. So she always thought of it; never as the King's. Now, suddenly, in the summer darkness it was hostile, the great bastions dropping to the sea and on the landward side the moat, still glimmering faintly in the last light and holding the pale reflection of two idling swans. But no drawbridge. Across the shining water her castle crouched, dark, monstrous and fearful.

"There is another way in, you know."

"No. There isn't. My father told me that only the King, through his secret passage, can leave or enter Kronborg without going through the main gate. And my father knows. It is his castle."

"Indeed?" the boy murmured. "I thought it the King's. You must remember that the old pile of Krogen was here long before King Frederick brought his architects to make Kronborg."

"Don't be stupid!" Fear sharpened her temper and raised her voice, and the boy raised his head to where the distant sentry walked the high Watch Gallery.

"Quiet," he whispered, "or the sentry will call the Guard. I tell you there is another way. Though you may not like it."

"I don't believe you."

"Come then."

He led her to the northwest corner of the castle. The trees grew close along the edges of the moat and, farther back, there were deep thickets of bushes.

"Give me your hand," he said and, fearfully, she put her cold fingers into his.

"I believe you really are frightened," he whispered, and there was mischief in his voice.

"No." She would have died rather than admit it.

In the depths of the bushes he let go her hand, and irritably she smoothed her hair, which had been pulled and dragged by brambles. She heard him grunt as if pulling something heavy, and then there was a scrape of tinder and a spark that died, followed by the steady glow of a small lantern.

"Quickly! Quickly! We cannot have the light seen."

She could not argue. Quickly as she could gather her skirts, she scrambled past a raised trapdoor, into an opening in the ground, and down a flight of steps. She waited at the bottom, turning her face from the black darkness ahead, watching him close the trapdoor and fighting to steady the sick trembling of fear. He must not see she was afraid!

But the icy hand she gave him in the darkness told him all she would not say, and for a moment he felt a pang of guilt. He had not thought she would really be frightened. He gripped her hand more tightly in his warm fingers, and led her on along the passage.

"Now you are underneath the moat."

She gasped and closed her eyes, waiting for the crush of water to come pouring through the ceiling. She stumbled on blindly with both eyes closed until she felt the boy stop. Then, cautiously, she opened them.

"Carl Adam! We are trapped!" Her hoarse terrified gasp rumbled like thunder along the echoing passage. Before them, the small light of the lantern lit a little circle on a stone wall. Dark and sweating with the damp, it closed the end of the passage.

"No. We are not. But this is what makes people think there is no way out save the King's passage."

He lifted his light as he spoke, and fumbled in the cracks of the dank wall. She did not see him do anything, but, "Ah," he said suddenly. Then the whole block of the wall turned upon an axis, and the passage stretched ahead again. After they had passed through, she looked back and saw that he had closed it.

They seemed to walk for hours, through passages so low they were forced to bend almost double; the icy water from the ceilings dripped onto their backs. It was a nightmare of wet and darkness and the cold smell of slime that smeared the walls. They came at last into great vaults where their little lantern made a pool of helpless light in a great threatening sea of darkness. But the boy knew where he was going. Hanne pressed beside him and struggled not to run.

"The casemates," he said to her. "Underneath the bastions. They held the soldiers ready to defend the castle in time of war."

After that, the dark tunnel seemed warmer and drier, as though they were coming slowly from a bad dream. At last he pushed a small door that opened behind the soft bulk of piled sacks of flour.

"We are in the cellar now, below the castle kitchens. Quiet, lest there is anyone about."

They waited for a time at the top of the cellar stairs, but the only voices were distant ones, in the rooms beyond the kitchen. Then, incredibly, they came out into the warm safety of the big room, with candlelight in copper pans, and the fire red with welcome under the bars of the huge grate. A few steps and they were in the courtyard.

"There." Carl Adam dropped her hand to quench the light. "Tell your father to put that in his plans. Did he not know of it? It is part of the old castle of Krogen that I told you about! Even your father can learn of his Kronborg from these of us who live here!"

His voice was light and the girl struggled to still her trembling. She was filled with guilt, excitement, relief, and

sheer terror from the dark journey underneath the moat. She blinked round her at the safe familiar walls and the jagged edge of the unfinished wing against the stars. There was light here in many rooms and from the Little Hall came sounds of music. It could not be so very late. Suddenly she became Hanne again, defending herself against the long evening of shared excitement.

"I thank you, Master Carl Adam," she said formally, "for your company."

In the darkness, Carl Adam snorted. "Quick!" he hissed unkindly. "Quick to your room before they catch you."

Her bedchamber was silent and empty, the bed warm from the copper pan that could not have been there very long. Their sitting room was empty also, her father's plans tidy on the table and the candles burning low. Stricken with guilt, she said her hasty prayers and scuttled into bed. There she sat anxiously, crouched between the vast curtains of her bed, her hands about her knees, waiting for the inevitable questions.

The first to come was her serving woman, who was herself a little flushed and flustered as she hurried into the room.

"You are late, Nina," said Hanne at a venture.

"I beg your pardon, Mistress Hanne. I am late, but I came earlier and you were not here. You were with your father?"

Hanne did not answer.

"I have not told a lie," she thought, and felt a sudden sense of excitement and danger as sharp as in the dripping tunnels underneath the moat.

Next it was her father, as was his custom, to bid her good night and see her candle out. It must be just the ordinary time for bed, she thought. What excellent good fortune!

"I'm sorry to have left you so long alone with your woman this evening," he said with his hand upon the door, "but the King needed me. Sleep well, my daughter."

"Sleep well, Father," she answered, and no more.

In the darkness she lay for a long time staring at the carved ceiling of her bed. The curtains were pale shadows at her sides and beyond the uncovered casement, the dark sky was still touched with icy blue. She thought back over the hours since the boy had spoken to her on the ramparts, and gasped to think that she had done more wrong things this evening than in all her life before. What would Aunt Elena say? But no one had found out. She had not told one single lie. Nor did she have to face a punishment. It was too easy to be wicked. Far too easy.

Stricken suddenly with guilt and panic, Hanne leaped from her bed and knelt on the cold wooden floor. Shivering a little in her ruffled nightgown, she went feverishly through all her prayers again.

Only when she was once more under her coverlet and sleep was creeping heavy underneath her lids, did she remember the sea-colored ghostly ship, creeping silently, without lights, across the evening sea to Sweden; and the intent abstracted face of the boy who watched her.

CHAPTER SIX

In the height of summer Hanne rode with her father to Copenhagen, to say good-bye to Aunt Elena, who was starting on her long journey back to Antwerp. The days were long and mild, the soft air brilliant with the ceaseless wind, and the vast sky was piled with the high gentle clouds of settled weather.

They were in no hurry, taking their way easily down the sandy pine-fringed road along the coast—the road which Hans and Georg had lost on that first bitter night. Their horses now ambled along on silent hooves between the deep-blue summer sea and the dusky sun-shot forests that rolled down gentle slopes to the very edge of the sands. There was little talk between them. Master van Maebergen was weary, hunched a little in his saddle with his head sunk in the mitered edges of his ruff. Hanne glanced at him often, but she was too shy to lead the talk, and so they rode in silence through a long golden afternoon, watching the sea widening beside them, and Sweden fading to the milky distance.

Her father wished for a few days of peace before the noise and bustle of the city, and they stopped in the evening at a little fishing village to the north of Copenhagen. It was coming to the hour that Hanne loved, when the blue light crept across the sea and all the colors sharpened on the land. The tiled roofs of a few rich houses gleamed red among the dark trees on the wooded slopes above the village and, lower down, the thatched huts of the fisherfolk clustered round the small harbor. As they approached, the candlelight of the little inn was warm on the cobbled court, shining through windows that faced out across the brilliant sea.

"Peace, Hanne. Peace," her father said, as he handed his horse to Georg and looked gratefully about him in the soft light. "Peace. Do you feel the silence? It almost hurts like a wound after the turmoils of Kronborg in these last months. Though what catastrophes they will achieve without me, I dread to think."

"Put it from your mind, Father." Hanne struggled for the right words to say; to interest and entertain this remarkable father, when she had him for a short time all to herself. She longed to make him look at her, to take his absent eyes from the sea, and to still the restless tapping of his fingers; above all to have him find her a companion. "Put them all from your mind and let it be a rest for you."

"Good holiday in truth, sitting in your aunt's parlor, suffocating with all the casements sealed lest they breathe a mite of summer air. Talking of what their good priest said last Sunday, and how he savored the excellent capon they gave him for his dinner; watching me all the time lest my rough man's boots foul the floors." He sighed. "But it is my duty. Elena has been good to you."

He wandered over to the wall that bounded the small harbor, and Hanne followed him. Peace was gone for the moment, the courtyard loud with the welcome of the landlord and the clatter of hooves, as Georg unloaded their baggage and Hans arranged the lodging for his master. Hanne was delighted to have him speak so to her about her aunt; as though he and she were different, and of an age. Her cheeks flushed their sudden easy pink and she tried to answer him lightly. Before she could find words, he leaned suddenly across the harbor wall and clapped his hands. Hanne followed him and leaned beside him, feet scrabbling in the stones that she might be high enough to see over. Immediately below them on the rocks that fringed the wall, two men were fishing.

"Ah—ha! Well done," cried Master Maebergen. "Well done. Surely a fine one!"

The scales of the struggling fish glittered blue-green in the light from the sinking sun, and the man who held it turned and screwed his eyes against the light to see who shouted.

"Fine enough, Master," he shouted back, and took a keen look at the clothes and aspect of Master van Maebergen. "You will buy it for your supper?"

"To be sure! To be sure! Bring it up."

Hanne watched in silence, and the round buttons down the front of her bodice pressed into her painfully against the wall, but she did not move. The man threw down the fish, and killed it expertly with the sharp blow of a stone. Hanne turned only when he came lazily, with no great haste, up the green and slippery steps to the harbor wall and gave the fish to her father.

"The little daughter will cook it for you, yes?" He pocketed the coins he was given, and smiled amiably at Hanne. She dropped her eyes at once and turned away, terrified that he might have seen recognition in her look. For it was, indeed, the same thick fair hair, the same handsome friendly face and the same voice. This man was the herdsman who had cried out in the dark room of Count Andreas. The evening was clouding over, and Hanne shivered in a sudden

cold wind from the sea. The man talked easily with her father, thanking him for his purchase, and forecasting the chances of fishing for the morning; offering the gentleman a boat if the day should prove fine.

Master van Maebergen watched him as he walked away, and dusted the scales from his hands after he had laid the fish carefully on the wide sea wall.

"Odd fellow," he said curiously. Her father had looked slight and scholarly in his dark suit with the linen sparkling at neck and wrists beside the great blond strength of the fisherman. And Master van Maebergen was not a small man.

"Odd fellow," he said again. "He spoke like no fisherman that I have known. Nor did he look like one, come to that."

He did not think long on it. He had traveled to all the capitals of Europe and met more odd fellows than he could bother to remember.

"Run and get Hans, child, to take the fish to the inn, or we will smell of it forevermore. Bid him cook it for our supper."

But Hanne did not run. She walked slowly, trying to watch her feet on the narrow harbor walk while her mind whirled in confusion and indecision. She had wanted something to talk of to hold her father's interest. Now she could run back and put into words all this dreadful certainty that was forming in her mind. There was the scene in the snowbound lodge; the flakes of gold on her horse's hoof; the odd remarks of the boy Carl Adam; and that ship, that evening.

Now she could run back, but what could she say? She held her skirts carefully clear of her feet, and looked down into the darkening water below her. What could she say?

——He is not a fisherman, Father. You are quite right. He is a pirate. The one that steals the amber for your doors and the gold for your ceiling.

That should arrest his attention and make him look at her. Her feet slowed and she almost turned, thinking of the rest of it.

——Count Andreas is his accomplice. He uses his hunting lodge to hide what he steals.

She shook her head in despair. It was too fantastic. Her father would not even listen. Count Andreas! Closest friend to the King, and one of the most popular men in all the Court, beloved by everyone, famed for his loyalty to the King.

And what of Carl Adam? She could find words for none of it, but least of all for the last impossible thing she had begun to suspect as the big fair man stood before them, swinging his shining fish.

Just once she looked back at her father, leaning with his elbow on the wall, his empty eyes on the sea. But her natural shyness with him was too great. She couldn't frame so monstrous a suggestion. Finally she turned and, without pausing, crossed the cobbled court of the inn in search for Hans.

When the cloudy dusk had darkened on the sea, Hanne faced her father in the candlelight across the clean scrubbed table and the soft blue and white of Copenhagen Delft. The private parlor that Master van Maebergen had arranged for them was old and small, but pine logs burned warm and sweet in the grate, and there were herbs and flowers to perfume the fresh rushes on the floor. The candles danced and flittered in great shadows on the raftered ceiling and, in the soft shifting light, Hanne picked at the steaming sea-fresh fish, and tried to entertain her father with the polite small chatter so carefully taught to her by Aunt Elena. He paid her loving courteous attention, but his absent eyes failed to clear, nor could his weary overburdened mind wrench itself from the problems of his castle.

In the public room of the inn, the fishermen gathered, coming in one by one to settle on the long benches, talking of their day's business as if they met in council. The man who had sold the fish learned the name of the fine dark-suited gentleman who had bought it for twice its value. He choked with delight and slapped his palms flat down on the greasy table, laughing until the tears ran down his face.

Master van Maebergen cut short his visit to his sisters, quickly wearied of all the things he had spoken about to Hanne. Well before the appointed time, he invented messengers from Kronborg to call him back. He kissed the tearful Elena good-bye and commended her to a safe journey, promising his presence before too long, back in Antwerp.

He and Hanne smiled at each other in unusual sympathy as they left the cobbled streets and waterways behind them and again took the sand road to the north. She looked at his kind face, and struggled once more to tell him what she knew, but she could not talk to him. She fell silent and then chattered politely of the beauty of the summer woods.

Both faces were soft with relief as they left the edges of the forest and saw the tall frail spires of Kronborg above its rosy walls that were lapped by the sea beyond the roofs of Elsinore.

Master van Maebergen was returning to the work that was his passion, anxious to hear all that might have happened while he was gone. Hanne was weak with relief. Now she could save her conscience by being back where she could watch and wait and find out all she might. If there was anything more to arouse suspicion, she could tell her father before it was too late, and any harm was done.

Below the Knights' Hall the new chapel was just reaching completion, and the King held its consecration in the first shining days of September, when the long blue hours of twilight had sharpened into early dusks, and the sea light that poured into the castle had lost the bright clarity of summer and fell now in hazy golden pools across the checkered floors.

The inside of the chapel was not finished but it had strength and grandeur and peace for the eye in the perfect rising of its walls and the smooth flow of its arched ceiling. It waited plain and empty, for the carving and the color and the gilding that was yet to come; sharp still with the smell of fresh cut oak, and hollow to the feet that walked up and down the marble aisle.

For the first time, on the day of the consecration, the trumpeters lined the fretted gallery of the slender tower before the Knights' Hall, splintering the bright air with their triumphant fanfare. Below in the courtyard, the massed people lifted up their heads and then turned in silence, as though a wind had blown them, to the gates below the King's rooms.

First came the priests in all their splendor, the sun gleaming on the pale silks of vestment and miter, and on the tall jeweled Cross that went before them. Behind them walked the King, and his fair Queen Sophia, their faces grave above their gorgeous clothes of State. In the privacy of his castle King Frederick liked to walk as simply as his subjects, but today belonged to Denmark and he passed between a sea of bowing heads and stiff skirts that spread like flowers on the gray cobbles. Next came their three children, the small Christian between his sisters, who looked carefully ahead with determined faces as they had been taught, walking straight and proudly and holding grimly to the restless fingers of their little brother. The dark angry little Prince of Denmark wished to walk alone and he was very near to tears.

Hanne watched from a place she had been given, close beside the chapel. She ached for the furious small boy, and longed to tell the little girls to let him go. The splendid glittering procession of the King's guests flowed past her into the church, and then her attention was caught by Carl Adam. Today he waited on his father formally, tall and handsome in a suit of rose damask, his doublet slashed with silver, a white plume in his velvet cap. He was growing rapidly and stood almost to his father's shoulder. Hanne was struck again by their likeness. She thought of a strange wild idea that had crossed her mind that time in the summer when she had passed a few nights with her father in the fishing village and had seen again the tall blond man from Count Andreas' lodge. She turned from it now as madness. In the last months, nothing new had happened. There had been no stories of fresh piracy, no odd behavior from Carl Adam, and Count Andreas had lived in the confidence and affection of the King. In the tranquil days of the late summer, there was no school, and while the King traveled through his kingdom, he left the castle life easy and idle in the shortening days and Hanne had come almost to forget her suspicions.

Count Andreas and his son moved into the carved doorway of the chapel. She saw her father, and Master Jasper, who had done all the beautiful woodwork of the chapel, and Master Thomas Frantzen, newly come to Kronborg, commissioned with the carving of the altar. Then it was time for her to go in herself, to the last humble corner by the door, which they had found for her as the daughter of Master van Maebergen, who had built it all.

She soon realized that she might as well have been outside. She could see nothing except the sea of jeweled head veils and the white icy lace ruffs above padded shoulders, packed between her and the Archbishop who spoke from the unfinished altar. The heat was so intense, even there beside the open door, that Hanne felt the perspiration come out under the headband of her coif; and the close-fitting stomacher of her best gown held her like a vise. The tide of heads in front of her began to haze and run together. Suddenly her hands were cold and she clenched them against the carving of the pew.

Through the rising darkness an arm came firmly round her waist and drew her to the open door.

"Best fall down outside, little Mistress," said a kindly voice. "It makes for less attention. Here, sit there a moment and take your breath."

She gulped and breathed as deep as she could and fought

the swimming sickness. Slowly, the cool air cleared her hazy head, and she blinked up at the round face of one of the castle servants who had stood rigid by the chapel door when the procession went in. She knew him well. He sometimes waited on her father.

"Thank you, Eben." Her voice was weak with relief, and fading panic. "That was almost a terrible thing that happened." Sick fright swamped her again at the thought of it, and weakness gripped her. She leaned back against the pile of stones where he had settled her.

"A moment," Eben said kindly, "and it will pass. You will be safe away before they come out. Here—where do you think you go?"

He grasped the arm of a thickset weather-beaten man who was striding past him at the same moment that two guards crossed defensive halberds at the chapel door.

"The King!" the man said urgently, as though he had no care of what went on. "I must see the King."

"Can you not see the King is occupied?" Eben's round homely face was shocked. "They consecrate the chapel." As if to prove him right, the low rumble of the congregation massed in prayer came clearly through the open door.

"Well, the Admiral of the Navy then. He must be here. Though the King bade us report all this to him himself." He ground one big dark fist into the other, and glanced in exasperation at the chapel. "Oh come, you are wasting time. The King or the Admiral!"

Eben spread helpless hands. "The Admiral also is in the depths of the congregation. You must just wait. And be *quiet!*"

"I cannot *just wait!*"

His voice rose, drowning the steady murmur of the Arch-bishop, and in the shadows of the chapel, shocked faces turned towards the door. The castle steward, in his cere-monial suit of black and gold, left his place of honor in the middle of the checkered aisle and came out, his old face creased with horror above his spotless ruff.

"What is this? What happens? Do you not know you dis-turb the King's prayers! And on such a day. Eben, call the Guard!"

"That's right," the man cried, and then made a great effort to lower his voice. "Put me in irons," he went on, hoarse and fierce, "while a pack of pirates runs another of the King's ships!"

The steward grew attentive, and Eben halted in his tracks.

"Pirates? The last one. The Odd One?"

The man nodded and small gold rings glittered in his ears.

"I think so."

The old man glanced at the chapel door and then drew the man aside, never noticing the girl who sat so close that her kirtle brushed against the elegant embroideries on his hose.

"Tell me."

"Sir. I am master of a galleon of the Navy. We were yesterday in the open sea beyond Hveen, when this ship closed on us in the twilight. Painted like a shadow, she was, and we never saw her come. Flying the Danish pennant, mark you. She must have mistaken us for someone else. 'Halt!' cries her master from her foredeck as she closes. Tall fellow he was, in a dark suit, with a shock of thick fair hair. 'Halt!' he cries again. 'Heave to. I have letters of marque from the Danish King, permitting us to search your ship.' 'Have you by God!' I shouted back, and ordered the men to the guns. But he saw his mistake at once and sheered away. We got only a shot or two at him. A clever devil of a sailor—took my wind as cool as you please. He outsailed me, fair enough, I say that."

The old man listening looked again indecisively at the chapel door, and his knobby fingers fiddled with his gold staff.

In the end he appealed to the sailor. "What should be done?"

"Done? Get the King! Get the Admiral! You know that nothing is closer to their hearts than catching this Odd One. Now the fellow is trapped if we are swift. Somehow he has got through the Sound and is in the Oresund. Get the Navy to seal the way out through the Baltic and out through the Belts. We have him then. But we must move now or lose him."

The steward moved.

"Somehow I will get the Admiral. Leave the King alone. Let him have his day of celebration in peace; we can tell him tomorrow. Now go to the Guard Room there by the gate, and wait for me—and hold your tongue on this to give the King his day. Tell no one. The Admiral will do with the Navy all that is necessary."

The banquet to commemorate the consecration was in the early evening. On the mighty hearths the logs glowed scarlet in the cool early dusk; and, in the long blaze of candlelight, the company sat down to dine. They were splendid and carefree in the gleam of velvet and the soft whisper of silks.

Smiling faces turned to each other above the sharp points of ruffled lace, and jewels winked on hands that reached for the finest foods among the spangle of crystal and the pale gleam of gold.

As they ate, a messenger pounded through the dark forests to the south, carrying orders to the Fleet at Copenhagen. In the King's name, the Admiral was determined that the last one of plundering pirates should be driven from the Danish seas.

: All day long, Hanne held her secret, adding one more certainty to the others. Over and over again the old worries came back to torment her. Who could she tell? And what could she tell them? Go to the King and brave that dark quiet face? Tell him that she thought his closest friend was in league with this last pirate who ravaged his sea and robbed his ships? Panic gripped her at the very thought. Go to her father? Today she had seen him only at a distance, remote and splendid in his crimson velvet with a gold chain, the King's gift, around his neck. He had been flushed with the torrent of congratulation that had flooded over him; his fair head bent in respectful attention to the distinguished guests. If she went to him, he would smile his absent pleasure and lay a hand on her and present her to the visitors; and then forget her. She sighed, and kept silent.

Later in the evening, the tables were cleared and there was dancing in the Knights' Hall. Light and music floated out of the high windows over the dark quiet sea while the shining company floated across the marble squaring of the floor. Long colored hose paced against the gentle swirl of shining kirtles and the light was soft on smiling faces under the splendid ceiling. Under the tall gem-crusted canopy of State, the King sat beside his lovely Queen, smiling down benignly on his guests.

The older children were permitted to watch and they sat together in a wide-eyed whispering group. But Hanne sat alone, disturbed and anxious, as she watched the calm handsome face of Count Andreas in the distance. In a gold-embroidered suit of amber satin he danced with a visiting princess. She had not seen Carl Adam at all, until he came suddenly and stood beside her when she was sitting in the shadowed alcove of a window. Only half her mind was on the brilliant gathering; the other half was on the sea outside, gleaming now in the pale light of a rising moon.

"You have not seen such a sight before, Mistress Hanne?" He spoke politely and formally as he pulled a stool and took his place beside her, calm and handsome as his father, in his pale rose and silver.

She looked at him and looked out again at the water far below the windows. Then, for no reason that she could understand, she turned back to him suddenly and blurted out what she had heard that day; that the Danish Navy was all out to trap the last of the pirates. Her confusion and bewilderment showed in her wide eyes. She did not know why she did it. Suddenly still, he looked at her for a long moment and then he got up and moved to the open casement to look down over the bastions to the sea. She watched him, her hands tight in the yellow satin of her lap.

"Hanne." He turned quietly from the window and his blue eyes were keen and searching on her face. "Hanne. Why did you tell me this?"

In the hall behind them, someone was playing the lute, sweet and plaintive as a throstle in the spring. She lifted her hands a moment and let them drop.

"I don't know," she whispered, "I don't know."

Tears of anguish and confusion started to her eyes. With all the long years of Aunt Elena's training to do right, she knew in her heart that he was the last one she should have told. But she could not help it.

After a moment he sat down again and took her hands in his.

"Hanne," he said, and his boy's face was strained and old with anxiety. "Hanne. I want you to help me. I can ask no one else. I must sail across to Sweden, and you know my boat needs two to sail it. You did well with it before, and I can ask no one else. *Please*, Hanne." His voice was hoarse and urgent.

"But——"

"Say only yes. Say only yes, I beg you. And ask me no questions," he added desperately.

For a long time her eyes roamed over his face as if she searched there for an explanation of what she did herself.

"I will come," she said at last. Carl Adam let go her hands and sighed. Through the open window a cool wind from the sea brushed their anxious faces and in the great brilliant Hall behind them, the music drifted into a fresh dance.

CHAPTER SEVEN

It was days before a chance came for Carl Adam to carry out his plan. There were long formal entertainments for the guests who had journeyed to the castle for the ceremony—a masque, a ballet, and a troupe of strolling players from England who, with their antic comedy, set the King rolling with laughter in his carved chair. He came down among them to praise them when they had finished, and bid them always welcome to Elsinore, urging them to come again. There was a long day of hunting in the damp autumn forest for the visitors. The last leaves were blazing on the beech trees against the dark pines, and the breath of the horses in the evening was cloudy with the first touch of frost.

Through the long formal days, Hanne had no chance to speak to the boy. She only saw him across the candlelit rooms, or as he passed attending his father in some procession through the long shadowed galleries. She had no chance even in the hunt, for Georg held her close and threatened her with the childishness of a leading rein if she strayed. Their eyes only met in the trampling bustle of the winded horses after a kill, but even in the dimness of the forest, Hanne could see the anxiety and tension that held him. Now the chase after the last pirate was common knowledge, and the girl watched Count Andreas. Surely if her suspicions were correct he should be as concerned and anxious as his son? Yet his easy smile was as relaxed as ever, and his habitual gracious manner as tranquil and unconcerned. Hanne fretted and brooded and worried and could make nothing of it, but for the first time in her thirteen years, her thoughts were never on herself.

Carl Adam had to wait until the last distinguished guest had clattered out through the arched gate in a flurry of horses and servants, while the trumpeters blew their strident farewell from the tower.

"Now," he said to Hanne urgently, edging up to her as the courtyard slowly cleared of the people who had come to watch. "We must go at once. Tonight."

"Yes, but Carl Adam——"

"What?"

"The wind. It has been high all day." She glanced up at the scudding clouds that raced above the roofs.

"You are afraid! Very well, I will go alone. I will manage."

"I am not afraid." She shook her head desperately. The last guest was barely over the drawbridge when the building was under way once more. She had to speak against the scream of winches raising the huge sheets of copper to the roof of the new wing.

"At least, I am not afraid of sailing with you." Secretly she wondered how her brief experience would serve her now, out on the racing waters of the narrow Sound. The wind had been keening through the castle all day with the cold promise of winter, and all the gusty strength of autumn.

"What then?"

The boy's temper was short, and his taut face began to grow angry. Hanne felt the old sick distress that overwhelmed her if anyone should disapprove of her.

"I don't know," she said, almost apologetically, "how to

leave my father and my maid tonight without a lie."

Carl Adam flared. "And it would not be *right* to tell **a** little lie!"

The familiar note of contempt was in his voice, and Hanne fought to hold her ground.

"No," she said, and would not look at his flushed face. "It would not be right." Now she lifted her eyes to his, and gasped for breath with her effort to be firm. It would be easier just to do anything he asked. Or to do nothing at all. "Nor is it right," she went on, "that I told no one else what I heard about the ship. There is much I have a right to know from you, but I haven't asked. But I *have* promised to come with you."

She trembled with the effort needed to rebuke him. She had never had to stand up to anyone before. No one questioned what she did because it was always what she had been told to do. Now she must think for herself.

"And I *will* come with you, but can't you tell me why we are going?"

She was rewarded by seeing his anger fade.

"Forgive me, Hanne. I am anxious, and my temper flies. I thank you for coming—but I beg you ask no questions."

They were in the way. Workmen shouted at them as they maneuvered the huge sheets of copper to the winches.

It was all too easy. Hanne had to tell no lies. Her father was closeted with his builders and did not come to the meal, and when she slipped away from the other children and came back up to her room, her woman was nowhere to be seen. She didn't stop to reflect on the ease of wickedness. As for how she would get back——! She seized her darkest cloak and slipped down the little-used stairs beside her room. Carl Adam was waiting.

"We will have to go through the casemates. The sentries would not pass us out at this hour!"

For all that it was her second journey through the long tunnel, she breathed the cool windy air in thankful gasps as the boy closed the trapdoor in the thicket at the other end. The boat was beached on a sandy spit beyond Elsinore.

"I dare not leave it at the castle slip. There is almost a full moon, and the watch could have seen us. They do not expect us to go sailing after dark on autumn nights." Hanne felt rather than saw him grin beside her in the fitful darkness that came and went as the clouds were torn across the moon. "They might ask us for the Sound dues," he said. He seemed more cheerful now that they were on their way, slipping through the woods along the shore below the small crowded lights of Elsinore. Anxiety faded with action and excitement and Hanne forgot to worry about how she would get back, and gave herself up to the secret thrill of running through the sheltered woods with the night air cool on her face, the stars in the tattered gaps above the pines, and the thunder of the sea below her.

The thunder of the sea! For the first time, she really listened to it.

"Carl Adam!" She grasped his jerkin and slowed him to a walk so that she could speak. "Carl Adam! Is it not very rough?"

The boy, too, paused to listen, and they stood for a moment in the silent wood, which was sharp with the smell of pine and spruce, and suddenly, in their own stillness, filled with the pounding of the sea. The boy paused so long that Hanne knew at once it was worse than he had thought.

"Shall we go back?" she asked.

"Go *back?*" It was as if she had asked if they should go to the moon that glimmered through the trees. Then suddenly his voice was desperate and sharp with urgency.

"Hanne. I cannot go back! Please do not ask me, but I must go on. You will be safe, I promise you. I have sailed far worse seas than this."

He went on without waiting for an answer, and she did not speak again until she was up to her ankles in the cold soft sand, as they struggled together to push the little boat into the water.

"May I even know where we are going?"

He paused on the other side of the boat, and in the unstable moonlight, she caught his grateful look. His voice against the surging sea was humble.

"You are very good, Hanne. I have asked much of you. And there is no reason you should help me. You are very good and kind."

She let go the boat in her confusion. All her life she had been good, and the most her aunt had ever said was that she did her duty. Now for the first time that she was really wicked, this boy looked at her as though he meant it, and told her she was good!

The cold sea broke across her feet in sudden agony. She gasped and lost her breath and forgot to think, as she struggled clumsily into the boat before the sea swept her away. Her shoes were sodden, and icy water from the ends of her skirts ran down her legs; but suddenly she did not care.

At first it was all right, as the boy had promised. The wind which blew from the north was strong and cold, and whipped through the narrow Sound, tumbling the sheltered tideless waters into racing waves. But the boy was competent, and handled his square sail dexterously, so that they tacked in the full strength of the wind and raced fiercely across the dark water.

"You see?" he yelled across the wind and the rushing of the sea and the thrumming of the taut sail. "It gets us there the faster!"

Hanne grinned at him, a sudden open delighted grin that Aunt Elena had never seen. He had given her the tiller and showed her a flaring watch fire to steer for on the Swedish coast. She felt the pull and power of the boat under the smooth wood in her hand, felt the need of all her strength to keep the bucking, racing craft straight on the water, as she kept her eyes on the distant fire. The leaping strength of the boat seemed to creep into herself, so that she wanted to laugh and shout aloud in her new-found power, as she thought back to the timid righteous girl of Antwerp.

He was quite right, she thought. I was a prig. If Aunt Elena could only see me now. She quickly pushed the thought of her father from her mind. Guilt was gone and fear, and she was lost in the enchantment of the racing boat and the thrumming wind under the tattered sky. For a forgetful second she looked at the clouds and eased her hand on the tiller. The sail thrummed with a new high note and the boat lurched to one side. Carl Adam fought to hold it.

"God's bones, girl! What are you up to! Get me back into the wind!"

Somehow, gasping and trembling, she did so, conscious of his half-seen angry face. I must remember, she thought, this has a desperate purpose for him even if it is only an adventure for me. She remembered briefly that she had told little Margrit there could be no adventure in Kronborg. She felt suddenly confused, as if she were two Hannes and she did not know which one was real.

The boat leaped suddenly under her, wrenching the sockets of her arms, and the sail cracked like a musket above their heads. Hanne ducked away from a drench of icy water; the tops of waves seemed suddenly twice as high. This was different. Carl Adam sensed her fright.

"The wind is changing!" he yelled. "Moving to the northwest! The hills of Sweden make it gust. And we are in the open now! It will be better later!"

It was not. Nor was there any chance even to speak as they struggled to keep the little boat on her course in the gusts that almost seemed to pick her up and hurl her across the sea. Hanne was cold now; excitement dead. Only fear kept her numb fingers on the tiller while wave after wave drenched her and the water ran in rivers down her sodden clothes—fear of what might happen if she let go. Every so often she was conscious that the boy turned and looked at her, but he did not speak; nor did she. She occasionally thought of her father.

The watch fire was clear and brilliant now, and the rising glow beckoned safety like a warm hand across the black heaving sea. As they grew closer to the Swedish coast, the gusts grew stronger, funneling down between the dark hills as if bent on catching the one small solitary craft that seemed to be afloat. The wind had scoured the sky of clouds and the moon shone down as cold and hostile as the sea itself.

Hanne was past words, and when the fiercest gust ripped the sail from top to bottom, she did not cry out, but clung dumbly to her tiller as the boat leaped and halted like a stag to the huntsman's arrow. She only stared up at the two flapping halves of canvas as they rattled in the wind, and felt her cold stomach begin to heave to the dead wallow of the boat.

"Keep her head to the sea!" yelled the boy, and she hoped she knew what he meant. She struggled to watch the moon-bleached edges of the piling waves and to keep her straight, but it was as if giant hands fought against her to pull the boat across the seas.

"Don't be afraid," Carl Adam yelled. "I know what to do."

He was scrambling in the water that swished around her feet.

"I am not afraid." She could hardly speak for her chattering teeth. "But I think I will be sick."

"Sick." He caught the one word and raised his head. His face was colorless in the cold moonlight and his dark drenched hair plastered flat. "You will not, my girl! There is no time. If you want to get back to Denmark, do as I bid you now. We cannot get to Sweden, but the drift of the wind is right to take us back to Denmark. Now come here."

His words came to her in broken fragments; he had been working as he shouted, prying the triangular floorboard from the bottom of the boat, and propping it up against the mast.

Then he scrambled forward, took the painter, and threaded it through the hole in the floorboard, struggling for balance in the wallowing craft.

"Now!" he yelled. "When I say Come, come quickly, and take this rope. Lie down in the bottom of the boat and hold it, tight—tight, so that the board is held against the mast. It serves as a sort of sail!"

She looked down appalled at the dark greasy sheen of water in the bottom of the boat.

"It is wet," she said foolishly.

"So are you. Now come!"

For a moment the boat yawed and slithered in the dark trough of a wave and heeled round broadside to the sea. Then the change was made. Carl Adam, with a firm hand on the tiller, quieted the bucking craft as he would a nervous horse, and Hanne, too astonished and bewildered to be frightened, lay facedown in inches of icy water, and clung for her life to the short end of rope, which tugged and chafed at her numbed hands.

She remembered little more about the night. It was almost as if she had slept, unbelievably, down there in the wet plunging darkness with the water slopping round her and the sea slithering and swishing past under her face. Carl Adam did not speak at all and she had no idea how much time had passed when at last there was a change. There was a rasp and a bump beneath her and the rope was jerked from her hands. She heard the sea wash up under the keel and wash away again in the hiss of shingle, and the boat was still. But she could not bring herself to move.

"Come," Carl Adam said beside her, and his voice was

hoarse and strangely gentle. "We are safe now. Get up, Hanne."

He helped her up onto the seat. She could not speak, but stared dumbly at the palms of her hands where the blood was drying in the salty agonizing tracks of the rope. She lifted her head and looked all round her as if the world were new. And it might have been. The wind was dying with the dawn, and the sea that chopped to the edge of the boat was gay and green, touched with the distant glitter of the first sun. To the west, the flat pine-fringed land of Denmark lay blue and shadowed, the sky above it still clouded by the night. But the hills of Sweden were sharp and black against the red dawn sky.

"We are on an island," she said, slowly and stupidly, closing her hands against the pain.

"Yes." He answered her eagerly in his hoarse exhausted voice, as though glad to be able to tell her anything; to talk to her at all. "I felt us still a dangerously long way from Denmark, so when I saw the lights here, I steered for them. It is Hveen, halfway between Denmark and Sweden."

She turned her tired head, and it seemed as if the night-mare had not come to an end after all, but was still going on, drifting into a less frightening dream. The green fields sloped steeply up from the sea, still dark with the shadows of the dawn, but the light was clear on the vast building that rose beyond. Hanne screwed her eyes. It must be a dream. It was monstrous, impossible, even to her who had been brought up with buildings. It reared itself above the fretted balustrades and terraces of formal gardens, the long façade not vastly different from her father's castle. But it was finished at the ends with mighty towers like cylinders, each one topped by a huge unsightly dome, and the center of the building was crowned by the biggest dome of all. Like an onion, she thought stupidly. She turned helplessly to Carl Adam.

"It is an observatory. The man who lives here, Tyco Brahe, is the most famous astronomer in the world."

Hanne tried to understand, but she could think of nothing clearly except the cold of the wind through her wet clothes, and the raw salt-soaked agony of her hands. She looked at them again and then looked at the boy.

"Hanne," he said, "I am sorry." He turned away from her and his eyes as he looked at the coast of Sweden were sad and despairing. "Can you move now? We must find someone to care for you."

He turned back and took her carefully by the wrist and helped her from the boat. They slowly plodded their way up the long stretch of cold sand, walking in the weight of their wet clothes as if they had grown old. The sun blazed suddenly from above the Swedish hills and warmed the sea to dancing blue. The enormous onion on the strange house was touched improbably with gold, and the sand was warm and yellow under their exhausted feet.

CHAPTER EIGHT

"But, Carl Adam!" Hanne whispered, awed and overcome by the strangeness of her surroundings. "What a most extraordinary place! Who did you say lives here? And will he send us home?"

She sat warm and weary in a strange room for the second time since she had left Antwerp. She was torn between the comfort of the great open fire and the hot meal she had just finished, and her desperate anxiety about her father. Carl Adam still picked at the crumbs on his platter and his eyes wandered round the painted walls and the rich damask of the hangings. The room was small and comfortable; it smelled sweet with the resin of burning pine logs and glowed with the soft colors of its furnishings. Through a fretted arch, it opened into far vaster rooms which stretched away beyond. Hanne thought sleepily that she must remember to ask her father why these Danes did not have doors. He had put doors in Kronborg. She was drowsy and her mind wandered; then she came to herself and frowned at the mystery of the charts and diagrams that mingled on the walls with portraits of men in ancient clothes, who bent over strange instruments. She shook her head. Carl Adam had not answered her.

"His name? And what did you say he is? And can he get us back?"

The boy lolled in his chair and his eyes moved lazily over the crowded walls and the statues visible through the fretted arch.

"An astronomer. A man who studies the stars. He is very famous here in Denmark. Some years ago he discovered a new comet in the skies, and the King gave him this island. Here he can watch the whole sweep of the sky without interruption. They call Hveen the Scarlet Island, and this palace is Uranienborg—the House of the Stars."

"How do you know all this?"

He was as sleepy as she was. He yawned and his tired head rolled on the red cushions, but his eyes were watchful.

"Someone who is interested in these things told me," he said, and his voice was careful.

She looked at him, and there was a silence between them.

"You still have not said his name," she went on in a moment. "Not that I understand it. And can he get us home? Carl Adam, we must get back. My father——"

"Brahe is his name. Tyco Brahe. I am told he is the greatest astronomer in the world today. I long to meet him."

Hanne blinked. She had seen all the stars she ever wished to see in the long night before. Carl Adam seemed almost happy to be here. She edged nervously in her chair.

"But can he get us back? Or mend our sail."

Suddenly the boy was angry. "Do not keep fretting to get back to Denmark! I had need to go to Sweden!"

She stared at his furious face, but his anger disappeared as quickly as it had come. He shrugged despairingly. "Forgive me, Hanne. Yes. We are quite safe here, and we will get back. The place is famous. Always full of visitors. There will be a boat, and someone must take us. You could not hold a tiller." He gestured at her bandaged hands.

"Someone is coming now!"

Both heads turned as one toward the fretted arch, but the firm steady footsteps coming through the corridors of rooms only belonged to a kindly old serving woman, who had come to tell them to sleep while their clothes were dried. They had seen her earlier when they first came ashore.

Hanne fought her heavy eyes. "But we must get back to Elsinore!"

The old woman smiled, and nodded her apple cheeks under the white frilling of her cap.

"There will be time for that. Now you will sleep." She clucked and fretted over them as she had done early that morning when the astonished servants had first brought them in, their clothes running with seawater. They drifted sleepily through the huge painted rooms with endless portraits and statues and inscriptions and clocks of every kind, but merely blinked at the splendor with heavy disinterested eyes. Behind them along the polished floors they trailed the long damask skirts of the furred robes in which they had been wrapped when the old servant took their soaking clothes. Hanne was not sure that she might not be dreaming already when she lifted her drowsy eyes to the ceiling of her bed and found it painted celestial blue and swimming with the constellations of the stars. At least, she thought as sleep claimed her, in this room there is a door.

It was evening when the old servant came to her again, and the dusk was sweeping over the skies beyond the casement. She had brought Hanne's clothes, dry and warm but a little shrunken, so that when she was dressed, her thin ankles stuck out long and comic from beneath her kirtle.

"It will do," the smiling old woman soothed her. "Now

come, my pretty. Master Tyco has bidden you both to sup with him. There is no one else here at the moment, and he dearly loves guests." She chuckled. "But never, I think, has he had two so young."

Hanne smiled back absently at the benign old face, but her eyes were on the darkness beyond the windows. "But I must go home."

"Yes, yes." The old woman soothed again. "Master Tyco will care for you. Follow me now, this way."

With that she had to be content, and anxious and nervous she followed the servant through the house. She would like to have asked what an astronomer looked like, but she was too shy. Her mind groped into the past, trying to recall old pictures on her father's shelves in Antwerp, their paint fading on the vellum of ancient books. She wished Carl Adam was beside her. Where was he? She paused inside the archway when at last the old woman stood back and motioned her into a room, and her astonished face could not hide her thoughts.

"Master Tyco, little Mistress." She was left to herself; she blinked and tried to speak but could not close her mouth.

"What is it, child?" The voice of the man beside the fire was amused and tolerant. "Do I have a pumpkin on my head?"

She gulped and groped for her shrunken skirts as best she could with her bandaged hands and dropped her curtsey. "Your pardon, sir. Your pardon. I just—— Well, I—— Well, sir, I thought you were an astronomer."

"So I am, child. So I am."

A yelp of laughter came from underneath his chair, and

the astonished girl fell silent once again, as she stared at the small creature who peered at her; he was only half her height, an old man with a silly face and the bright motley garments of a jester.

"So I am, child. So I am," he cried after his master, and his voice was deep like a giant's.

"Quiet, Jebb," said Master Tyco, and then bade her tell him how she thought he should look.

Lamely, scarlet to the roots of her hair, she tried to tell him, realizing too late that the pictures she had been thinking of were of the old practitioners of magic. But no old picture, she wanted to cry out, and no magician could be as strange as you really look.

Master Tyco Brahe was not very tall, but he looked thick and heavy in a huge padded robe of crimson velvet crusted with gold and silver embroidery. The flames of the candles were reflected in a jeweled pendant round his neck. He had no hair at all; his head was large and round and bare as some monstrous egg, but his mustachio swirled and curled across his face and its waxed points stuck far out beyond the sides of his cheeks. The bridge of his nose was missing, but had been reconstructed with gold and silver that gleamed in the candlelight like a third huge eye in the middle of his face. Jebb, the dwarf crouched under his chair, was grumbling and chittering and jangling his fool's bells; and at his feet sat a small black smooth-haired dog, as ugly and arrogant-looking as Tyco himself, with a ruff as crisp and spotless as its master's around its neck.

Hanne jumped again with nervousness as a clock behind her began to chime the hours. She turned and watched in

fascination as small figures flew through open doors and marched with restless jigging round the dial. Through the whole great house the hour was echoed on clocks that chimed and boomed and whistled, and a small one in a corner that tinkled through a tiny tune. She turned back speechless to the big bald man beside the fire.

But the eyes in the strange proud face were not unkind, and soon he had pity on her and bade her come into the room and take a stool beside him. The room was like all the others, painted and gilded, filled with pictures and statues; but this one also held books. There were more books than she had ever seen, ranged along carved shelves with the light soft on their leather bindings. As she moved across to the fire, she brushed against a globe so vast that it stood taller than herself; it was made of silver, and carved, she saw in her quick glance, with the stars. A globe of the heavens!

"And who is your father, child?" he asked her as she timidly settled on the opposite side of the fire, her eyes a little fearful of the dwarf.

"Julius van Maebergen, sir. He is at Kronborg. He will be very anxious about me. I beg you, sir, to send us back at once."

"Back at once," rumbled Jebb.

"We will arrange it. Master van Maebergen, who rebuilds the old Krogen? So! I have a distinguished guest."

Hanne blushed, embarrassed to be thought of as important.

"And the boy? Is he your brother?"

"Oh, no. He is the son of Count Andreas of Rosenborg."

"And what were you doing out on so wild a night?"

Hanne bit her lip and smoothed her shrunken skirts around her ankles. "Sailing," she said lamely, and wished Carl Adam would come.

On the egg-like face across the fire, the eyebrows lifted high above the gleaming nose. "Sailing?" he said. "I see." And mercifully asked no more.

"Sailing," growled Jebb and shook his bells.

Carl Adam came in, as comic as she was, in a shrunken doublet that did not meet his breeches. She saw his eyes widen and grow dark, as they flicked from the metal nose to the dog and the grumbling dwarf, but he politely showed no surprise. Hanne envied him his long Court training, and blushed again for her own awkwardness.

The meal was long and rich and the table laden with the best of Delft and sparkling with crystal and silver. The astronomer drew the boy out on all he knew about the stars and his arrogant eyes grew kind at Carl Adam's eager interest. Hanne looked from one face to the other and wondered again where Carl Adam had learned all he knew, for she was sure Count Andreas had never sailed the northern seas. Under the table, Jebb growled and grumbled and begged for scraps from his master's hand, and the smooth little black dog sat erect in a chair of his own.

"Now," said Master Tyco when at length the meal was over and darkness had fallen beyond the leaded windows. He spoke to Carl Adam. "You would like to come and see my observatory?"

"Sir." The boy could not get up fast enough from his velvet chair. Hanne followed more slowly. Master Tyco moved over to the wall, where a strip of tasseled damask hung from the ceiling. The children watched him, and, with his eyes on them, he pulled it.

A servant bowed in the open archway of the room a moment later. "You called, sir?"

Hanne stared at Carl Adam and he stared back at her, and the astronomer watched them both, his big round face bland with amusement.

"Yes," he said to the servant. "I called. Bring me my scarlet robe for the observatory."

"But, sir! You didn't call." Carl Adam had found his voice.

The eyebrows lifted above the curled mustachio.

"Did I not? Why did he come then?"

He delighted in their confusion and would not explain to them. He allowed himself to be helped by the servant into a robe of even greater magnificence than the one in which he had eaten the meal.

"The stars are always worthy of my best," he said portentously. "Tonight, boy, I will show you the observatory. I have a laboratory, too, where we study the properties of metals. We blow our own glass for our experiments, and make our own paper so that we can print and record our findings. No, Jebb, you will not come now."

Carl Adam was bright with enthusiasm, but weariness was creeping over Hanne. Her hands hurt her and she wanted to go back to her father. She dragged her feet as they followed the astronomer on his stately progress through the ornate galleries of the House of Stars. Young men paused to bow to him as he passed through the big rooms, then they turned back to bend once more over sheets of parchment.

"My students are making a calendar of the stars," he said, and Carl Adam would have lingered. "Each star we record is charted here, and then carved in its exact position on the great globe in the library. You can see it all tomorrow. Come now, for the moon will rise soon, and then the stars grow dim."

They came to the bottom of a circular stair in a tower, and the weary girl remembered the palace as they had first seen it from the sea. Could that really have been only this morning? It seemed like another life. A gilded statue of a dancing nymph stood at the bottom of the stairs. Master Tyco glanced at the children and a look of mischief crept across his face again. He touched the statue as he passed, and at once she revolved as though she was dancing, and music tinkled up the winding stair. Blandly he walked on up, planting his feet firmly on every step, and the children looked at each other and followed in silence.

To Hanne, the observatory was nothing but a bewildering mass of things she did not understand and was too tired to care about. One section of the dome was taken out and the air was cold, here above the sea. The vast round room was full of instruments, huge structures of brass and oak and silver, which Master Tyco showed to Carl Adam. He grasped their big handles and turned them, and the two of them talked eagerly as the structures moved.

"Sextant," she heard them say, and "Arc," and "Minutes," and many other strange words. They understood each other, but Hanne could not bring herself to listen. She leaned against the open wall and looked at the spyglass in its cradle, as she wondered miserably about her father. Carl Adam seemed to have forgotten the need for getting home, and she could do nothing herself. She was very near to tears and wondered how distressed her father was. She was desperately tired and, underneath the bandages, her hands were paining her afresh. She listened to the boy's delighted exclamations and the deep rumble of the man's voice and raised a disgusted face to the sky. Stars! They were well enough beyond the window. How was her father? A prank was one thing, but not for the world would she cause him grief. Perhaps Aunt Elena was right, and it was wiser always to be good. She caught a smatter of the conversation between the boy and Master Tyco.

"—more than ordinary knowledge," the astronomer was saying. "Who has taught you?"

"My father," said the boy at once, and there was no hesitation in his voice, only fierce pride.

"He must have considerable knowledge." In the dim light, the nose gleamed brighter than the face.

"He has indeed." The same note of pride.

"Count Andreas af Rosenborg. I have never heard that he was interested in astronomy. Perhaps we could persuade him to sail from Kronborg and visit with me here. I would be most interested to meet him."

There was a long, silence, and after a while Master Tyco looked curiously at the boy, who did not answer.

"Perhaps," Carl Adam said, and his voice was dead.

There was an awkward moment and then they began to talk again, and Hanne leaned against the wall and longed to be allowed to go to bed if she could not go home. She was nearest to the stairs, and it was she who first heard the faint murmur of voices that came echoing up the round tower from far below. She got the impression of delighted greetings and one dominating voice that answered. Then came a step on the spiral stair, around and around, firm and even and unhurried; and a voice called out well before the footsteps reached the top, "I have come to interrupt you, Tyco, my friend! Put away your stars and bring out the wine! I have been away too long!"

There was light enough to see the delight that spread across the astronomer's round face, and the way in which the boy turned sharply from the spyglass. Carl Adam stood rigid, his gaze fixed on the head of the stairs and his face frozen in disbelief.

"Lars!" cried Master Tyco as the man came up, and his voice was warm and pleased like the voices had been at the foot of the stairs. He came forward with hands outstretched. "Lars!" he said again.

"*Father!*" cried Carl Adam in the same instant. Incredulous pleasure lit his voice but he did not move from where he stood beside the spyglass.

Tyco halted between them, hands still outstretched; the metal on his nose flashed as he looked from the man to the boy.

"So!" he said.

Hanne, too, looked from the boy to the man, tall and easy almost to arrogance. She looked for the third time at the wide good-humored face and the thatch of thick fair hair. A herdsman? A fisherman? What was he this time? But whatever he might pretend to be, she felt that in her heart she had always known he was Carl Adam's father.

CHAPTER NINE

How did you guess?"

The following morning they stood on one of the terraces which leveled the sloping land from the House of Stars. Carl Adam leaned on the marble balustrade and gazed without interest at the peacocks that strutted and spread their splendid tails on the grass below. He turned to Hanne for her answer.

She put up a hand to snatch her cap against the rising wind.

"I don't know," she said doubtfully. "I don't know. But I honestly think I knew from that first night in the hunting lodge, although at the time I thought nothing. I was just confused. I only thought about it afterward. You were not like each other, but there was something in the way you stood." And in the way you looked at each other, she thought but did not say, with some warm closeness she had never known with her own father. "Then when I saw you look so like Count Andreas, and everybody said he was your father, I did not know what to think." She turned to him, her face grave and troubled. "You have much to explain to me, Carl Adam."

"I know." The boy stood up from the balustrade and kicked at the gravel with the toe of his shoe. "Come," he said. It would be easier to tell her if they were walking and he did not have to stand and face those steady eyes. "We will walk down to the harbor, and I'll tell you on the way."

Hanne looked back at the house, monstrous against the

sky with its domes and statues and fretted balustrades.

"What about getting back to Kronborg? We *must* get back!"

"As soon as my father is awake he will arrange it. He sat up late last night with Master Tyco." He grinned suddenly as though he shared their pleasures. "We will be back at Kronborg today, Hanne, never fret."

With that she had to be content. The House of Stars stood on the highest part of the Scarlet Island, and from there to the north end, the land sloped gently down, set beyond the formal gardens with all the mass of buildings belonging to the Observatory. In the distance they could see the little harbor and the road which wound down to it through the sloping pastures. Beyond that lay the woods and thickets and green spaces of Master Tyco's game preserve, where his famous guests enjoyed their hunting with his pack of hand-picked hounds.

"How much do you know, Hanne?" The boy was careful. He was not yet sure whether she realized that his father was the pirate they called "the Odd One."

"All of it, I think. Except to know why." The sky was clouding over as the wind increased and the sea beyond the green fields was gray and choppy. She began to tell him all she had seen and put together: his arrival with his father in the hunting lodge on the first night of the snow, and the report of the sea captain that his ship had been plundered on that same night; the finding of the gold leaf on her horse's hoof after the spring hunt. Here Carl Adam looked at her in silence and amazement, but did not speak. His own anxiety, she went on, to get to Sweden when he heard the Navy was mustering everything to catch the last pirate.

"You thought all this, Hanne, and yet you came with me?" The boy looked at her with curiosity and she looked away uneasily. She, herself, had no idea why she had done it. She didn't answer him.

"You wanted to warn your father, didn't you?" she said instead.

"Yes."

"He is the last pirate, isn't he? The one they call 'the Odd One.' "

"Yes." The word came short and unwillingly.

"Have you warned him now?"

"Yes."

"And what did he say?"

Carl Adam's unhappy face suddenly broke into a grin.

"He laughed. He told me where the Danish Navy might go for all it troubled him. But I had better not tell you that."

Hanne was shocked. "I think you had better tell me everything." She was as prim as when she first came from Antwerp.

"Yes." The grin faded, and the boy's face grew defensive. "It is not his fault he is a pirate," he almost shouted. "He was driven to it. My father is a good man. I'll tell you," he added more quietly.

The small road sloped gently down through the damp grass, and the last leaves, torn from the few bushes, ran and rustled round their feet. The wind caught their cloaks from behind and almost ran them down the slope, and it was difficult to talk.

"My father was a sailor in the wars against Sweden," Carl

Adam gathered his cloak close round him and tried to keep beside her. He was quieter, but his voice was still resentful. "My Uncle Andreas was a soldier."

"Your *Uncle* Andreas?"

"Yes. He is my father's elder brother. When the long wars ended, my uncle had caught the King's eye on the battlefield. For him, honor and preferment. My father had fought just as bravely and all his men with him, but for him nothing! Nor for his men! Nothing!" His voice was rising again, harsh and angry against the keening wind. "Sailors in hundreds were left to starve along the quays in Copenhagen. The King was done with them but my father would not see his own men starve. One way or another, the King should keep them." He grinned a little again. "He only robs the King's ships."

"He stores his booty at your uncle's hunting lodge?"

The boy stopped and the grin left his face. His eyes were horrified. "Hanne. My uncle is the King's friend!"

Hanne shrugged hopelessly. There was an impossible mixture here of good men who did evil things. She could not follow. "The gold leaf in my horse's hoof?" she asked helplessly.

"My father has a hideaway in the forest, not far from the hunting lodge. I was in his ship that snowy night."

"How? You live at Court."

"Oh I simply rode away to join him. My uncle did not know and he was very angry. But I am my father's son, and I must choose the life I lead. I am not ashamed of my father."

Hanne still groped. "But why did *you* have to sail to Sweden to warn your father? Why did Count Andreas not go, since he knows all your father does?"

They were walking slowly again, the girl puzzled and confused, the boy almost circling round her as he tried to make her understand the strange double life that he led.

"Hanne, he is the King's loyal friend. I *told* you. But he is also my father's brother." His face grew sober. "It is hard for my uncle; he is the King's man, but he loves my father. He knows what he does but does not speak of it and he would never *help* him." His blue eyes were sad. "They long ago agreed that if my father were in trouble, Andreas could not help him. So I had to go to Sweden, and my uncle would have stopped me if he had known."

"And if you were caught with the pirates?"

The boy shrugged and his eyes lit up with the casual light that so labeled him his father's son. "Then I would allow my Uncle Andreas to disown me too."

Fine words, thought Hanne, but her slow cautious mind felt it might not be so easy. More likely that the boy and his gay brigand father might drag the Count down with them, even from his high position.

"Ten years a pirate," she said, "and never caught. He must be very clever."

Carl Adam shone with pride. "He is. The finest sailor on the northern seas. But not ten years. Five years ago it grew too dangerous; there were many pirates after the wars, and at that time the King hounded them all down and heads rolled like apples in the square at Elsinore. My father took his crew and went off to fight somewhere in the south of Europe. Three years ago he came back—tempted by all these rich ships coming in and out of Kronborg. It is only since then that I have seen him enough to know him."

"Why?" Hanne's question was short and sharp. There was much to be explained, and a lot of it did not seem to make much sense.

Carl Adam was defiant and embarrassed. He did not like to admit his admired father had cared nothing for him when he was small, but Hanne had helped him, and she deserved his honesty.

"I told you," he said, "my mother died when I was born. My aunt Ose, wife to my uncle Andreas, was then alive and they had no children of their own. My father," he spoke with difficulty and would not look at her. "My father had no use for a small child, and never came near me. My aunt Ose died when I was seven, and Uncle Andreas and I have been alone since. But three years ago my father came back into these seas close here beside us, and sought me out, since I was grown. But Uncle Andreas persuaded him that as far as the world was concerned, things were best left as they were, although he has never stopped me from seeing my father. My Uncle Andreas is a good man," he added thoughtfully.

Hanne was still thinking—of a summer evening and her father buying a fish beside a harbor wall. "What was he doing in Torbaek?"

The boy laughed delightedly. "Master van Maebergen took him for a fisherman! Hanne, my father does not *hide*! He is a trader up and down these coasts and everybody knows him. He takes only the King's ships and always in dusk or darkness, so he is never seen. But there is a small cove in the Swedish hills where he lies when he needs to be secret and that is where I was going. I thought after he had been seen by the Navy, he would be lying low awhile. But he is not troubled. He says they had no chance to see him properly."

Hanne was silent, trying to absorb it all and understand. They were on the lower land now, coming close to the little harbor, but they had lost sight of it. Here there was shelter and quiet, though the wind still moaned above the sea. There were a few cottages, crouching under the slope of the land, safe like the little boats from the strength of the northern winds.

The boy watched Hanne's face and found it full of doubt and disapproval, set in the old expression of self-righteousness and virtue.

"He could not help it, Hanne! He is a good man! He has done this to keep his crew who fought so faithfully with him through the wars. The King would not keep them. He is good!"

He spoke with all the ferocity of one expecting disbelief, and his dark blue eyes were angry and uneasy.

"He is just as good as your father," he shouted suddenly, and the girl stared at him in astonishment. "You think so much of him!" he went on furiously. "Oh, you are not so bad now, but when you came!" He made a gesture of disgust. "Stalking around the castle with your head in the air as though we were dust beneath your feet because you were the daughter of Master van Maebergen!" He was shouting again now, worked into a rage by remembering the months he had watched her so jealously. "Right from the beginning you angered me and made me want to bait you; so pleased with yourself! Don't you know your fortune! It is easy to be

proud of a father such as yours, but I am proud of mine too!
Proud! Proud! Proud! He is as good as yours, I tell you, prig
that you are!"

He turned away abruptly, but not before she had seen the
glint of tears on his cheeks. She stood quite still and silent
and her own cheeks were a faint unhappy pink. Was that
how she had seemed to him—and to other children? While
all the time she spent herself in an agony of effort to be
perfect enough to please this remote brilliant father of her
own. In the few brief moments in the hunting lodge and in
the little while they had talked the night before, she had
sensed between Carl Adam and his father something she had
never known; something that made her ache with loneliness
and longing and bite her teeth on jealousy so bitter that it
shocked her. Was he really suffering during these days when
people talked so ill of this unknown pirate, and he had
walked with Count Andreas, and never shown it in his calm
and pleasant face?

She went over to him after a time, to where he picked
furiously at the bark of a tree beside the road. She touched
him on the shoulder and felt it hunch under her hand.

"I am sorry, Carl Adam," she said simply. "It is not really
like that."

There was no more she could say now. The boy turned
and smiled at her with difficulty. His face was white and
strained.

"I am sorry too, Hanne. We will talk no more of it. This
is the harbor now, I think, and I will show you my father's
ship. She lies off because the harbor is very small."

It was very small, built of loose piled stones, a mild protection against the open sea for the few small craft which lay there. Hanne picked her way along the top of the wall behind the boy, tightening her cloak against the wind that took them here in its full force, so that she would not be whirled into the sea. Her mind still boiled with the whole strange story and even more with the boy's wild outburst of rage. She paid little heed to what was around her.

"There she is," Carl Adam had recovered and his voice was warm again with pride and pleasure. Hanne steadied herself against a stanchion at the harbor end and looked to where he pointed.

"Oh," she said. "She passed us that first night you took me sailing."

"Yes," he said, and no more. His eyes were on the ship.

She was a caravel of strength and beauty, painted in the blue of the deep sea and the pale green of the shallows, her galleries and the carving all along her sides picked out in white. Sea-colored, the man had said on the day of consecration; but she was too brilliant for this gray unfriendly sea. Yet she rode the waves with the same light grace as she had driven that evening before the summer wind.

"Carl Adam, she is *beautiful*," said Hanne, and was glad that she could mean it. "But what are they doing?" The ship was noisy with the clang of hammers and her decks were bustling with activity.

"We cannot see it, but she is damaged on the other side. They shot at her, remember? My father says it could be dangerous if the sea ran high. They can repair it here while he visits Master Tyco." He grinned again. "He told Master Tyco that he rammed a harbor wall."

"And Master Tyco believed him?"

"Master Tyco has known my father a long time, and knows his seamanship. His eyebrows would have hit his hair, had he any, but he said nothing."

Hanne spoke again after a long pause, her eyes fixed on the ship. "Does Master Tyco know?"

Carl Adam glanced at her and his voice was as awkward as her own when he answered. They could not yet speak of it easily.

"Who knows what Master Tyco knows?" he said.

She had been watching the vessel, as it rode there so easily, summer-colored on the slate-gray autumn sea.

"Carl Adam," she said again suddenly. "She is beautiful," she peered across the cold water, "but I cannot see her name."

The boy looked at her and smiled and his face was happy again. "She has no name now; it is painted out. But do you not see her colors? She is the *White Twilight*."

"Of course." Her voice was soft with pleasure. What else could she have been called, this lovely ship?

"I named her for my father," the boy went on, and pride and affection were warm in his voice. "For does she not, I told him, creep across the northern seas?"

They looked at each other and laughed. The cold wind plucked at their hair and the sea leaped in towers of spray above the harbor wall. They were friends again, jealousy and uncertainty forgotten.

"Carl Adam," said the girl urgently, turning to the gray distant coast of Denmark as if she had for a time forgotten it. "We must go home."

But when they got back into the House of Stars, and sought the two men in the library where they pored over the celestial globe, Carl Adam's father shook his fair head.

"I'm sorry, Mistress Hanne. I understand your concern for your father." He moved over to the casement and looked down on the sea. There was a white cap now on every racing wave, and the wind moaned like a troubled spirit round the house. "No small boat of Master Tyco's can go out today, the sea is too fierce. My own ship cannot sail out into this before she is repaired. She is damaged just above the water and it will be difficult to repair it even in shelter, in this sea. Patience until tomorrow, Mistress Hanne, and then I will get you back."

"*You* will get me back?" The words burst out of her without courtesy.

"Get me back. Get me back." Jebb beat his bells against the silver globe and Hanne stared in anguish from Carl Adam to his father. If he had only looked like a pirate it might be easier; but surely pirates did not wear dark elegant suits of heavy silk with diamonds in the buttons of the doublet, and fair hair groomed and shining above a ruff of finest lace? He smiled at her easily from where he stood with an elbow on the mantelpiece, and his dark gray eyes had the same look as his son's. Hanne felt herself blush as though all her thoughts were spelled out on the polished floor between them. She looked desperately at Master Tyco and got no help at all. He twirled his long mustachio and his eyes were vacant above the gleaming nose. Carl Adam grinned like his father, and Jebb leered at her from beside the silver globe; even the dog seemed to grin at her above his ruff.

It was Carl Adam's father who rescued her; just before she burst into tears, he moved from the fireplace and put an arm around her shoulders.

"You will be quite safe with me," he said, "little Mistress. I will see no harm comes to you and get you safely to your father." His eyes signaled to Carl Adam to tease no further, and he led Hanne to a velvet chair beside the fire. "Now tell me about your father," he went on. "Tell me about all he does in Kronborg. I hear stories of great things."

Hanne sat rigidly on the edge of her chair. It was one thing when she was not sure he was a pirate, but now she knew; knew he was a robber and a thief, and that many honest men had died because of him. Fiercely she tried to remember all this but as the man talked it slowly slipped away from her into some hazy distance where it no longer mattered. She felt his kindness flooding over her as the sun flooded the dark floors in Kronborg. It was the same warm kindness with which he smiled at Jebb as the fool rolled about his feet; the same warmth that brought an answering glow into the face of everyone he spoke with. Charm crinkled his gray eyes, and his smile was easy and open.

The blue-green flames of driftwood danced in the open hearth and the day closed in in the long, shadowed room. Hanne slowly leaned back in her chair, relaxed and content; all anxiety vanished in the company of the tall man who sprawled opposite across the hearth, his son at his feet. Jebb had crept close, and crouched with his head against his knee, his vacant fool's eyes fixed on his face and his bells forgotten in his hand. Master Tyco had long gone away, but the little dog had stayed and now he jumped onto the man's lap, and he was not put down. An idle hand lifted to caress his ears and the small animal sighed with pleasure and laid his head against the friendly arm and slept.

The two children talked and the man listened, and laughed and listened again, and talked to them as though they were important, and their faces glowed as they looked at him. The logs fell crumbling on the wide hearth in showers of colored sparks and outside the wind tore and battered at the shuttered windows. Through the great house the clocks chimed and boomed and tinkled on the hour and darkness thickened in the corners. The silence of peace and safety fell round the hearth and Carl Adam looked across at Hanne from beside his father's feet.

"Did I not tell you he was like this?" asked his proud contented eyes.

But when Hanne was alone in her bedchamber where the old servant fussed and tidied her before the evening meal, she began to think and fret once more. The warm kind presence of the man was gone, and she began to be troubled again about what he was. It was one thing while she only suspected; now she knew. The years of Aunt Elena's training nagged her conscience. What should she do?

"I beg you, Lise," she said suddenly to the old woman, "be quicker with my hair. I must see Master Tyco."

"But you have seen him today, my pretty."

"I want to see him before the meal, before the others are there. Please, Lise."

The old woman shrugged her ample shoulders and her gnarled fingers moved more quickly through Hanne's long hair.

"There—and I have freshly goffered your cap for you." Lise was delighted to have a child to care for, and fussed and muttered with pleasure. Now that Hanne had made her decision she could hardly wait for the cap to be put on her head, and the old woman stared after her in disappointment. When she reached the parlor and found the astronomer alone, she had little breath left to speak to him.

"Master Tyco," she gasped and curtsied. "May I speak with you?"

"Speak with you," growled Jebb, but Hanne could not see him. So voluminous was the robe that Master Tyco wore that evening that Jebb was hidden under the stiff purple folds; he peered out from underneath them, his restless fingers stroking at the deep border of fur.

"Master Tyco," she began again.

The mustachio twitched and the face was growing a little irritable. "Yes, yes, child. Come to it."

"Come to it." From beneath the purple skirts

Hanne glared at him. It was difficult enough. Jebb glared back with his red-rimmed eyes and shook his bells at her.

"Master Tyco," she burst out, too disturbed to care. "What do you know of Carl Adam's father?"

"Carl Adam's father," rumbled Jebb.

The eyes above the gleaming nose had taken on a watchful look. "What should I know of him, except that he is my friend?"

The voice was cool, but Hanne was past caution. Someone had to tell her what she must do about this, for she could not decide it on her own.

"Master Tyco." Her bandaged hands twined themselves in

the folds of her kirtle. "Master Tyco, did you know he is a——."

Tyco Brahe rose so suddenly that the dwarf was tumbled over his back with all his bells a-jangling, and the startled dog fled to the corner of the room. He seemed in that moment to the terrified Hanne to be as tall as a giant, and away above her the fierce mustachio quivered with threat under the fantastic nose. But the voice when it came was quiet and definite.

"Mistress Hanne. You may have heard that I am of noble birth. The highest. I am no true *Master* Tyco. I could have lived my life in wealth and idleness like all the other noblemen. But I left because it sickened me. In that world you only asked about a man's position, never of his character. You chose your friends for the label of their name. I left it."

He paused and Jebb crept back under the chair. "I left it. I left it," he rumbled. He felt the tension in the air, and beat angrily at the legs of the great gilded chair.

"Silence, Jebb. On my island, Mistress Hanne, I have many guests." He puffed himself out to his fullest size and his face was smooth with pride. "Kings, princes, nobles. I entertain them all, but I still claim the right to choose my friends as I will. Lars Nielsen—" Hanne started at the name. Was that what he called himself? "Lars Nielsen has been my friend for a long time. I know him as an astronomer. I know him for his character. I love him, Mistress Hanne. I ask no more. I ask no questions. About *anything*."

His eyes lifted above her head and he moved from the fire. "Ah, Lars. You are come. I am afraid there will be no stars to watch tonight. Come to the fire, the year grows cold."

Deliberately he stepped past Hanne, and laid a welcoming arm round his friend's shoulders. Lars smiled and threw an arm round him in turn. When he sat down and stretched his legs to the blaze, Jebb crept close to him. The dog came back from the corner of the room. Lars reached out a foot and kicked a stool beside him; he smiled at Hanne.

"Come, child," he said, and in a moment, Hanne came. The sharp eyes of Master Tyco watched her from across the fire, and then he, too, smiled at her and sank again into his chair.

CHAPTER TEN

They went before dawn next morning, when the first gray hint of light was creeping across a quiet sea; and Hanne had found no courage to say that she did not want to sail back with a pirate. Master Tyco bade them good-bye at the great carved door of the House of Stars. Hanne watched him as he clasped his old friend by the hand, and in the shifting light of the candle which he held, his smooth round face was grave and sad. He called Carl Adam back as the boy was leaving him.

"Son," Master Tyco said, and put a hand on his shoulder. He seemed to choose his words with difficulty. "There may come a time when, like myself, you wish to leave the vanities of the Danish Court. You know a great deal about the stars already. Remember, boy, remember, if you wish it, that Tyco Brahe will always have a place among his students for Lars Nielsen's son."

There was a moment's silence in the small pale light, and through the open door the wind off the sea was chill with the coming dawn. The two men looked at each other across the boy's head, and Lars laid a hand for a moment on his friend's arm. Then he turned out through the door into the dark morning.

"You will forgive me." He came to them later where they sat together on a coil of rope as the *White Twilight* slid in silence from Hveen, out towards the breaking day. They sat beside the mended hole, and the new timber reeked still of its fresh paint. "You will forgive me if I do not land you below the walls of Kronborg. The King might wish to speak with me, and I have not the time to spare His Majesty." For a moment the gray eyes were hard and then he grinned at his son who grinned back at him, and Hanne blushed and did not know what to say. "I will have my men row you ashore in the small bay below Elsinore. You can go back safely from there, and it is not in sight of the castle."

They were close to the coast, tacking for the bay as dawn broke, when they saw the galleon. She was making for them from the south, the scarlet of her pennant a tiny point of color against the pearly sky. Long before she could hope to be in range, a threatening cannon exploded from her bows and the smoke was dark against the morning.

"She knows me better than I thought!" Carl Adam's father leaped to the poop and his crew were running to obey his stream of orders. They were almost within the slight sheltering arm of the bay, where the southern headland would give a few brief minutes of protection. Hanne stood bewildered in the turmoil of men who snatched off the hatches of the ship and handed up to each other as fast as they could work what looked to her like sheets of painted board. She had no time to think. She and the boy were rushed to the lower gallery as a small boat was swung over the side to the sea. The moment the ship was sufficiently steady, Hanne found herself clinging to a rope ladder, swinging perilously above the little boat, so small and far below her. There was no time to be frightened. Almost without thinking, she was down in it, urged by Carl Adam from above and caught by the two seamen who waited below; then they were rowing like madmen for the shore.

"Carl Adam." She clung to the side of the boat that leaped with the pulling on the oarlocks. "We did not bid your father good-bye."

He threw her a grim glance. "No. There was no time. Was there time for him, Gert?" he asked of one of the men.

The man nodded, too exhausted to speak. "Just," he said.

Hanne looked from one to the other and did not follow what they were saying, and then she looked back at the *White Twilight*. Something strange was happening to the ship. Hanne jerked around as the small boat grounded in the shallows.

"*Run!*" cried the two men. "*Run!*"

The children ran; floundering through the shallows and up through the heavy sand in their sodden shoes, never pausing until they were safely inside the shelter of the forest. Then they turned around and Hanne's eyes grew wide and disbelieving. The boy laughed softly in the green shadows beside her.

"There was time," he said.

The galleon of the Navy was just rounding the small headland, boarding nets hoisted and the crew lining her rails for a capture. An unrecognizable ship lay tranquil in the bay, higher in the poop than the *White Twilight*, blunter in her lines, and all her upperworks painted in black and scarlet above her sea-green keel. Two of her seamen dug indolently for bait on the sands below the forest, their small boat drawn up below them on the shore.

Hanne watched in pure astonishment, unaware of the desperate tension and anxiety of the boy beside her. The galleon sheered across close to the moored ship. There was shouting between the two vessels, and from what must have been the *White Twilight*, willing arms pointed around the next arm of the shallow bay. She was already unfurling her sails as the Navy vessel pulled away, and the bait diggers swiftly gathered their belongings on the shore.

She felt Carl Adam let out a breath of relief. "It is broad daylight, and the day before him," he said. "Pray God he may get away. The master of that galleon must truly be a fool."

"But, Carl Adam," Hanne found her voice at last. "How was it done?"

"The false ship? An ancient trick and an easy one, as long as no one comes too close. It would deceive only a fool—I am amazed he got away with it in broad daylight. The false boards are ready built to slot above the rails and on to the top of the keel. It is simple, even in a short time."

"But they would surely be found if the ship were searched?"

The sails of the *White Twilight* were rapidly shrinking away towards the Swedish coast, and the galleon had passed out of their sight around the curves of the land to the north.

"Oh yes." Pride and self-confidence rang in Carl Adam's voice. "But no one has ever come close enough to search my father. Now, Hanne, we have our own troubles. We have to get back to Kronborg and settle on the tale that we will tell."

The girl turned to him sharply with her old air of self-righteousness, to say she could tell nothing but the truth. Carl Adam had looked back again towards the sea. His bright self-confidence was gone suddenly and he leaned his head against the rough trunk of a pine and stared after the vanishing ship. Hanne looked at the loneliness and fear that swept his face and her words died away unsaid. She knew that when it came to it, she would tell nothing that could harm him or his father.

It was quite easy to conceal everything, and without a deliberate lie. After his first warm embraces that held nothing but relief, her father faced her across the litter of his table in astonishment and disbelief.

"You went sailing?"

"Yes, Father." That was no lie.

"On such a night! And why at night at all?" She was silent.

"Whose idea was it?"

"Carl Adam's." This was true and he would say the same. "But I wanted to go, Father. I could have refused."

She was not as frightened, or horrified at herself as once she would have thought. It was a long time since she had not wanted to climb the Trumpeters' Tower in case she displeased her father; other loyalties had come to pull at her.

"Sailing! On such a night," he said again. "You might have lost your lives!"

He looked at her with honest amazement on his thin fair face. This was as hard to believe as if he had discovered his gentle daughter had suddenly grown horns or found six fingers on her hands. For a moment Hanne's heart lurched with the sick knowledge of his grief if indeed she had been drowned. She had come very close to it; for the first time in her life, she thought of his feelings and not only of her own. She moved quickly to the table and laid her hand on his.

"I am sorry, Father. I would not have wished to grieve you."

The unexpected gesture of affection puzzled Master van Maebergen no less than the rest of the story. What had happened to his cool remote Hanne, who put up a shy cheek for a kiss on the right occasions, and nothing more? He looked at her in perplexity, and for once his plans lay forgotten on the table.

"And who brought you back, you say?" He struggled to sort out the long muddled story she had poured out on her return. Sailing in a half gale? And at night. Tyco Brahe on the Scarlet Island? A man who sold fish? The whole rigmarole did not make sense.

"I told you, Father. That seaman, you remember? He sold you a fish one evening in Torbaek in the summer. He was on the island and he brought us back." Again it was no lie, but looking at her father's confused bewildered face, Hanne felt that she was torn in two. He let her go in the end, without punishment, because, he told her coldly, he could not believe such madness would ever be repeated.

Hanne left him, far more humbled and upset because she had deceived him so easily than because he had rebuked her. It would have felt better somehow if he had had her whipped.

Carl Adam had not fared so well.

"I was lucky to get away without a flogging," he said morosely. "My uncle is not your father. I did my best, but he suspects where I have been and he was furious that I brought you into it. He wonders now how much you know." He sighed. "I make trouble for everyone. But in truth it is not my uncle's business if I want to see my father!" His dark face was truculent.

Hanne was gradually finding it easier to be firm with him. She no longer cared whether he found her a prig or not if she knew that she was right.

"It *is* his business, Carl Adam," she said now, "as long as you are living as his son. If you want to claim your father, then you must go to your father, and stay with him."

The boy looked at her and his eyes were angry and dismayed. They were standing on the bastions on the quiet walk below the South Wing, and there was no sound but the whistle of the wind around the castle walls and the soft pounding of the sea below them. He pushed back his hair from his eyes and stared out across the sea as though it might tell him what to say. He was not yet ready for this decision.

Hanne did not press for the answer. "Has he punished you?"

"I am confined for a month inside the castle."

She looked at him a moment. "The casemates?" she asked hesitantly.

Now his face was angry; the misery had gone from his eyes and there lay there some of the old contempt. "All right, Mistress Virtue! I promise you I won't use them. I will honor my uncle's punishment. After all, as you tell me, I am still living as his son!" He flung away from her and the wind took his cloak, dark against the soft red of the sandstone walls.

And honor it he did, though in every idle hour he could be found leaning on the rampart walls, staring at the sea.

The wet and windy autumn drifted late into another long dark snowbound winter. No news came of the capture of the last pirate for all that the Danish Navy had sealed off every exit from the Oresund, and the watch was doubled across the Sound between the castles. Gradually it seemed he was forgotten, and people talked of other things. Watching him now with understanding, Hanne saw Carl Adam's strained face slowly begin to relax, until he took on a measure of his old self-confidence. He grows sure, she thought, that his father has beaten them again. She remembered the warm kind companion of the fireside; and she remembered the men who had died that he might steal; and she did not know what she hoped herself. But at least Carl Adam should not lose his father because of her.

She was gentle and affectionate with her own father because she was deceiving him and hated it, and he watched her with a new interest. He wondered if his pale prim tongue-tied Hanne was going to blossom into a different person after all. He had hoped for so much in taking her away from the narrow rigid company of his sister, and bringing her to Kronborg to a wider life. It began to seem as if, after all, he had been right.

It was Count Andreas who grew old during these months, and his dark handsome face thinned about the cheeks and wore a look of permanent anxiety. Like Carl Adam, his eyes were often absent, as if he had a decision to make and could not make it.

The cold winter dragged on into spring. Only late and slowly did the white fields begin to patch again with green and the empty trees take on the yellow haze of new leaves. Spring came with a rush in the end; the country was loud with the sound of running water and suddenly the fields were full of cattle, brought out from the barns to the first lush pastures of the season. In the town of Elsinore people looked upward at the beat of wings above their chimneys and smiled happily at those who had shaken their heads in despair and said it was too late; that the storks would never come.

The excitement of the season was reflected by the excitement of the people inside the castle on the Sound. They smiled and talked in groups in the soft new sunshine in the courtyard that was slowly being cleared of the larger rubble of the building. When the King passed by, they bowed and smiled their pleasure, for he was wise and popular and strong. And the dark heavy face of Frederick himself was warm and gratified.

His dear sister monarch, Elizabeth of England, had so honored him as to bestow on him the Order of the Garter, the most illustrious honor her country could present. The Ambassador of England was traveling from Copenhagen to present him with the insignia here in his new castle.

He summoned his chamberlains and nobles and planned the most brilliant reception that his new castle had yet seen. From his tower room he looked down across the courtyard and he was well pleased. The castle would be worthy of the great occasion. The new West Wing was complete—"The Queen's passage to the Knights' Hall" they called it, but he thought of it as "Sophia's Wing," built so that his Queen might walk in peace to the Chapel or the Hall rather than have to walk in all weathers across the crowded court. The fresh stone was pale and beautiful in the spring sunshine. Kronborg; he had named it so himself; it was his castle.

It was crowded to its immense walls for the occasion. All the State rooms in the West Wing were occupied, and all the new rooms that had been built beside the chapel. Attics meant for storerooms were filled with trundle beds to house the servants, and Hanne's maid slept on the floor beside Hanne's bed. Food poured into the castle kitchens, and down in the packed stables grooms slept beside their horses, glad of the shelter and a heap of straw. The vast building was filled with the comings and goings of the most illustrious personages of Europe, who moved slowly through the great sea-lighted rooms and watched each other, behind their smiles, like brilliant birds of prey. The long dark passages were filled with their servants, who ran everywhere and seemed forever in a hurry, and who constantly fell to blows over the importance of their masters.

The presentation of the Order of the Garter was made on the last evening of the festivities, and Hanne stood at her window and looked across at the blaze of candlelight along the casements of the Knights' Hall. She had been forbidden to leave their apartments. For these few days the castle belonged only to the King. She had watched all the press and flurry in the courtyard down below and, had heard the trumpets blare out to welcome the English Ambassador. She longed to see the brilliant ceremony in the great Hall. She could see they were dancing now. The music floated out through the open casements, into the summer evening that was drifting blue into the twilight. She could see the guests moving in a pavane. She caught a glimpse of the King, not dancing but sitting below the canopy of State, a smile on his dark face and a broad dark-blue ribbon across the pale satin of his doublet. She craned her neck a little. The ribbon bore a great brilliant star: the new Order!

She saw Count Andreas, as he passed in the dance, and thought how thin and old he had grown through the winter. She realized, with a little stab of guilt, that she had not really thought of Carl Adam's real father for weeks, caught up as she was, in the general excitement. She had not seen the boy, himself, for days. He would be in there now, waiting on Count Andreas.

She turned from the window and rather hopelessly went over to her bed; there was no chance to sleep. The white twilight glowed beyond the copper roof, and the music poured all night from the Hall. She could hear her maid tossing on the pallet on the floor. She did not fall asleep till dawn, when the guests had at last gone to their apartments and the exhausted musicians lay down on the floor where they had played. At daybreak the servants crept about, extinguishing the pale points of the dying candles, and the sea-light was cold across the empty floor.

Later in the day they all departed. Hanne leaned her weary head against the casement and wondered how they could dance all night and then set off to travel, many of them halfway across Europe. She shrugged and yawned and smiled with tired pleasure at the last fanfare from the trumpeters sharply outlined in their scarlet coats against the deep blue sky.

Then it seemed as though the stones of the castle sighed and settled down to recover from the turmoil.

She slept that night the deep heavy sleep of weariness, and when she first heard the cannon it was only as a huge terrifying intrusion in her dream. The second ball woke her clearly, but her maid was at the casement before her.

"Mercy! Mother of God, Mistress Hanne, what is it! Shall I get your father?"

From beyond the Queen's new wing, the thunderous explosions seemed to shake the great stones of the castle. An answering thunder came from far away, muffled by the sea. It was the great guns of Karna.

"It must be—it must be the cannon on the bastions. It must be some ship trying to run the Sound. It must be . . ." Her eyes flew open wide. "Nina! My clothes! Quick—my clothes!"

It was not yet dawn, but the strange black dusk that goes before it. The sky above the Queen's wing was bright with sudden scarlet at each crashing roar and the air was acrid with the smell of smoke. The cannon of Karna flashed like an echo across the dark water and the courtyard was loud with the sound of running feet as lights sprang on in the casements of the King's rooms.

"Quickly, Nina, quickly!" Voices were shouting under her windows but she could not hear what they said. Outside her bedchamber she ran into her father.

"What is it, Father? What is it?"

"Some ship running the dues, no doubt. There is nothing to be afraid of." Her father was calm and inclined to be a little irritable at being disturbed. He looked in surprise at her distraught face.

"It is nothing, Hanne," he said again, but she had not waited to listen to him.

Carl Adam caught her as she rushed through the passage

of the old tower, and made for the big windows of the Hall.

"Have you seen anything?" she cried.

She did not ask him what he thought it was for she knew and he knew. He waited through another roar and in the red flare of light she saw his desperate face.

"The bastion gates are closed. I was heading for the Hall."

They found a place in the press of people at an open casement; furred robes had been flung over nightgowns and hair was uncombed; all were a little annoyed to be disturbed but were ready to enjoy the drama down on the dark sea. The dawn was creeping into the long room and light was growing on the water. Their eyes were blinded by the flash of the cannon and it was a long time before they could see anything in the dead gray light.

It was as if Hanne and Carl Adam were alone. Fear and anxiety held them separate, away from the cries of "There she is!" and the gasps and the excited laughter. They did not wait beyond the moment that they saw her, outlined against a cannon flash from Karna; a phantom ship that tacked desperately across the Sound with sails flapping on her broken spars. The light was gone, but they could still see the dark shadow on the sea, and the fountains of water around it from the cannonballs. But the brief glimpse of the ship was firmly printed on Hanne's mind. The *White Twilight* was broken, running in the shadows for her life, merely the ghost of the beautiful ship that had ridden so quietly across the summer sea.

"Oh, Carl Adam," she cried in anguish.

He already had her by the hand, and eased her through

the curious crowd until they could run the length of the marble floor and down the small corner stair. In the courtyard the boy stopped, and the silence of the cannon was like a pain.

"She is through," he said. "They cannot fire straight across the Sound, in case they damage ships at mooring." He ran on again. Hanne did not ask him where they were going but followed him until they had got their horses and were riding across the moat, and toward the green fields. Away to their right, the crippled ship made all possible speed in the growing light.

"Carl Adam," she said. "You must say where we are going. You know I will come."

He looked at her as if he did not see her, as though he had brought her as something necessary, as he might snatch up a crossbow and give no thought to it. Then his eyes cleared a little and he blinked at her.

"Forgive me, Hanne. I know where he will take the *Twilight*; where they will run for shelter. I am disobeying my uncle but even if I can do nothing, I must see that he is safe. He has a chance. He has full sail, except for the broken spars, and the ones that follow him must get sail *and* get out to catch the wind. He has a chance."

They did not speak again, but rode steadily side by side through the forest. In the trees above their heads, the birds sang a welcome to the lovely day and the bright beams of the sun were straight and sharp as spears through the dark pines. Fear and anguish seemed impossible on such a morning were it not for the stricken ship below them on the sea. They could see her clearly now where the trees thinned, and how much she was damaged; the white galley hung in fragments and the high poop was a heap of timber.

"She is slowing," said the boy. "Pray God she can keep on." He looked back incessantly at the white sails that crowded the sky to the south. "We will reach the bay before her."

And she was not in sight when at last they left the forest and pulled their winded horses to a stop. They sat above a small bay where the sea rolled on a soft white beach and grass-grown sandy cliffs sloped down to it from the darkness of the trees. Somewhere above them a cuckoo called and called and called again in the first ecstasy of summer. Hanne looked at the peace and gentleness of the little bay and sick panic struck her for what she might be going to see. She longed to turn and dig her heels into her horse and never stop until she was safely back in the shadowed room at Kronborg, face to face with her father so that she could tell him everything. She wanted to see no more and know no more of this terror that had grown too large for her.

The *White Twilight* came round the corner of the little headland.

The crew were already struggling to lower a small boat from the damaged rail.

"Why don't they swim for it?" the boy cried furiously and then fell silent, for he knew why.

When at last the boat was in the water, they lowered a man carefully in a rope sling, and even at the distance the children could see the blood dark on his clothes and the cloth about his head. Hanne looked in sick dismay at the boy beside her. He did not take his eyes from the boat, but

without a word slid from his saddle and began to scramble
down the sandy cliff. When he reached the shore he helped
to pull in the boat. There were only five men left in it.

They laid his father in the fine soft sand and gathered
around him, and there was a long empty silence, broken only
by the quick rushing of the sea beside them and the cuckoo
calling from the hill above. After some hesitation, Hanne,
struggling with her skirts, climbed down to join them below.

"Ah, young Master," said the eldest seaman, and his own
arm was gaping with a wound and crusted dark with blood.
"I am sorry. He was alive when we put him in the boat."

The boy's eyes had not left his father's face, untouched
for all his dreadful wounds. It had the same easy serenity
that had marked it in life.

Carl Adam looked up. "Go," he said, with all the author-
ity of his father. "Go at once, all of you. There is nothing
here to wait for." He glanced at the headland to the south
"You have only a few moments. Now go. It is what my
father would have told you."

He didn't look after them as they scrambled up the sandy
hill and disappeared into the trees. In the end Hanne
touched him on the arm.

"We, too, Carl Adam. We must go."

He looked at her then and his eyes were unseeing but
some part of his mind knew there was sense in what she said.
He looked once more at his father as though he felt there
must be something he should do, and then, walking like a
boy asleep, he turned and followed Hanne back to the
horses. As they rode into the forest, she looked back once at
the bay; it was almost as they had come to it, but with the

beautiful ship grounded in destruction and Carl Adam's father dead down on the sand. Blinking rapidly, she realized that she had felt none of the fear she had so dreaded, or the horror, only a strange sense that she had grown much older. Through the trees they saw the white topsails of the pursuing ships.

For a long time the boy did not speak but stared straight ahead of him and saw nothing. Hanne did not try to speak either but kept quiet at his side until his stony face began to crumple and tears threatened his unseeing eyes.

"It's not *fair!* Why should he die? He was a good man, as good as any of them!"

Hanne sighed and struggled desperately for this new strength of hers. She did not quite understand herself, but she knew that she must hurt him first and then he would feel better. She took a deep breath.

"No, Carl Adam," she said, and her voice was hoarse with the effort. "He was not good."

She felt the boy stiffen with outrage beside her.

"Oh," she rushed on, "he was many things that made people love him." She remembered the warm safety of the firelit room on the Scarlet Island; the dwarf who crept to his feet and the small dog sleeping on his arm. "I would have loved him, too, I know. But Carl Adam, how could he be good, doing what he did? Men died so that he could steal. Good men. And do not say he did it for his sailors. One cargo would have kept them for a lifetime! He *liked* to be a pirate! Oh, Carl Adam," she cried with sudden wisdom, "remember him truly, and then you won't grieve so much!"

The boy looked at her for a moment in a blaze of anger

and then he laid his head along his horse's neck and rode in silence, his face turned away from her. When he sat up again the blind look was gone. He was white now with misery and grief, but no longer angry.

"So my Uncle Andreas always told me," he said slowly, "but I refused to listen. In my heart I knew that he was right, but I wanted my father to be like other people. You are right, Hanne—it will be better to remember him as he really was." He gave the faint glimmer of a smile. "You are always right, Hanne."

He sighed again after a while.

"That was why you so annoyed me when you first came to Kronborg. I was jealous of you. You were proud of your father and so secure with him. I wanted to be proud of mine."

Hanne shook her head in silence.

"But somehow," Carl Adam went on, "I always wanted to tell you about him. Perhaps that was why I made so many mistakes with you. I never gave myself away with other people."

There were voices ahead of them in the forest and quickly Carl Adam brushed his hand across his face and straightened in his saddle. Half the Court seemed to have ridden out with the same idea as themselves, but fortunately, they had not been as quick.

"We did not see much," the boy called to them as cheerfully as he could. "She is aground in the bay at Kildekrog, and a dead man on the shore. I thought Mistress Hanne should come back."

The party rode on, eager to see all they could, and a

woman's voice cried clearly that Andreas af Rosenborg's son looked half dead this morning, and she really was against the keeping of young pages up all night when there were revels! The querulous voice died away and they were alone again in the silent forest.

Near Kronborg, Carl Adam spoke again.

"I will bid you farewell now, Hanne, at the gate. I will not see you again."

"Farewell?" She looked at him with the cold sense of more sadness yet to come.

"Yes. Farewell. I have long decided on this. Remember, Hanne, I have waited all the winter for today."

Hanne thought with guilt of the months when she had forgotten the danger to the man who called himself Lars.

"I am going to Master Tyco as a student," the boy went on. "He asked me to, remember?"

Hanne remembered; and remembered, too, the sadness of Master Tyco's face in the pale candlelight as he bade farewell to his friend, as if he, too, waited for today.

"Of course," was all she could say. And sadly, she watched him go under the echoing archway.

Her father came to find her in the evening, in the deep window of her room, as in her yellow gown, she leaned against the white wall with her tired eyes on the distant sea. He came in quietly and she did not turn around; half across the room he stopped and looked at her.

"Hanne, my daughter," he said suddenly and tenderly, and his voice was full of surprise and pleasure. "You are growing up. And growing beautiful." He took her hand and looked at her again, and Hanne knew at last that he really saw her. Not for being good, she thought ruefully, and for a moment, the tears were hot and difficult behind her eyes, but she managed to smile and thank her father, and he moved in beside her in the deep window, still with this new look of pleasure and interest on his face.

"The Court hums with news," he said. "Have you heard it all?"

"I have heard nothing, Father. I have been asleep all day."

"Ah yes. The pirate ship was taken this morning. After the shooting stopped they found her empty up the coast with a packet of dead men. One of them was on the shore—must have rowed himself there before he died. Nothing more. That at least is the end of the piracy, and of the Odd One. But of your friend Carl Adam and his father, have you not heard?"

Whatever her sadness, it was a strange new delight to talk in this way with her father.

"What of them?"

"The boy is going to Tyco Brahe of Hveen, to study astronomy. Did he and Master Tyco speak of it when you were there? He has already gone, they tell me. And the Count Andreas has announced he is giving up Court life and retiring to his estates in Jutland. The King is very angry, but no doubt the Count Andreas does not want to live in Court without his son."

Does not want to live in Court with his conscience now that he no longer needs to care for the boy, thought Hanne. Yes, it was the honorable thing for him to do, and the best thing for Carl Adam to have gone to Hveen. For Lars, it was better that he died as he did, in battle, escaping the headsman's axe. All three were good and kind in their own way, and yet each had had a part in wickedness. She laid her head against the cool glass. It was all so confusing; she had so struggled to be grown-up, to impress her father, and she had been quite sure that she knew what was right. But this world that she had blundered into with Carl Adam was the real, hard world of being grown-up, where right and wrong were all mixed up and you had to keep choosing between them. Never again would she be in a hurry to be grown-up for it was not as easy as she had thought. She would just be Hanne, and she would be thankful to be a child with other people to tell her what was right and wrong.

Sick with relief, she turned again to her father, and although her face was still sad, her smile to him was warm and loving. Someday soon, when it would harm no one, she would tell him the whole unhappy story of Carl Adam and his father. It would be quite easy, for she would no longer have to search for words to talk to him. She smiled again in the contentment of being safe, and her father smiled back and wondered again what shadow had touched and so changed her. Then he put an arm around her shoulders and looked across the glinting copper roofs towards the sea.

"Have you noticed, my daughter," he said, "how strange the twilights are here in Denmark? Long long into the night, and such a color. Almost white."

Hanne gazed across the bleaching sea toward Hveen.

"Yes, Father," she said. "I have noticed."

The correct name of the architect who rebuilt Kronborg was, of course, Antonius van Opbergen. As I was unable to find out any personal details of his life or appearance, I gave him a fictitious name and made him a fictitious character. This leaves Tyco Brahe as the only main character who is possessed, to the best of my ability, of his own name, habits, and appearance.

After completing school in England, Madeleine Polland planned to be a painter, but circumstances changed her decision. During World War II she served for four years with the W.A.A.F. and it was then she first began to write—short plays and entertainments for her friends. After the war Mrs. Polland was married, and a home and two children kept her occupied until 1960, when a friend suggested that she write a book. She did just that, and CHILDREN OF THE RED KING was selected as an honor book in the New York *Herald Tribune* Spring Book Festival.

Since then Mrs. Polland has written several books for children: BEORN THE PROUD, also a *Herald Tribune* honor book; THE TOWN ACROSS THE WATER, chosen by the New York *Times* as one of the 100 Best Books of the Year; and THE QUEEN'S BLESSING. A dedicated interest in history has made the setting of the author's books authentic —Mrs. Polland was born in Ireland, but moved to England at an early age and has never ceased to explore the heritage of both countries.

Mrs. Polland visited Kronborg Castle three years before she wrote THE WHITE TWILIGHT which, she says, "I think was written from 'feeling' for a place—I had it in my bones for years before I wrote it."

Mrs. Polland's husband is with the University of London. A recent family move from London to the country will, she hopes, "provide a great deal more peace and quiet for writing."